For Mrs. Clarke—my principal,
my mother, my best friend

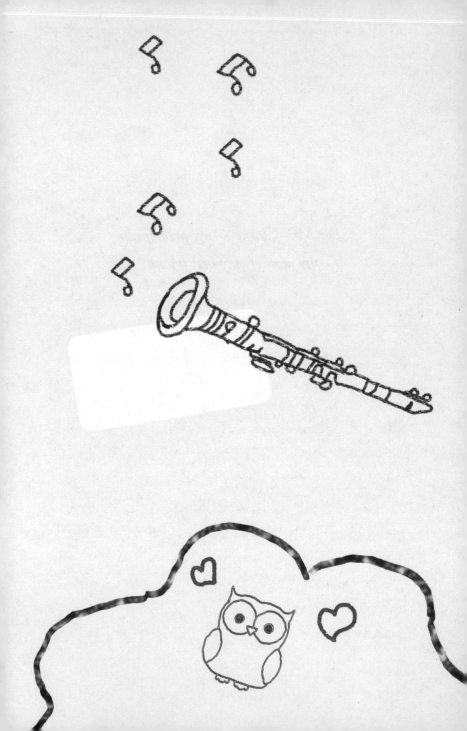

CONFESSIONS FROM THE PRINCIPAL'S KID

Robin Mellom

Houghton Mifflin Harcourt
Boston   New York

The text was set in Adobe Garamond Pro.
Cover design by Lisa Vega
Interior design by Lisa Vega

The Library of Congress has cataloged the hardcover edition as follows:
Names: Mellom, Robin, author.
Title: Confessions from the principal's kid / Robin Mellom.
Description: Boston ; New York : Houghton Mifflin Harcourt, [2017] | Summary: Allie
West finds it challenging to make new friends and stay true to old ones as she navigates
fifth grade at a school run by her mother. | Identifiers: LCCN 2017001204
Subjects: | CYAC: Middle schools—Fiction. | Schools—Fiction. |
Friendship—Fiction. | Principals—Fiction. | Family life—Fiction. |
BISAC: JUVENILE FICTION / Social Issues / Friendship. | JUVENILE FICTION /
School & Education. | JUVENILE FICTION / Social Issues / Bullying. |
JUVENILE FICTION / Family / Parents. |
JUVENILE FICTION / Social Issues / Values & Virtues.
Classification: LCC PZ7.M16254 Con 2017 | DDC [Fic]—dc23
LC record available at https://lccn.loc.gov/2017001204

ISBN: 978-0-544-81379-3 hardcover
ISBN: 978-0-358-55481-3 paperback

Manufactured in the United States of America
1 2021
4500831124

This Starts with a Spitball

I wish I could say it starts with a bouquet of daisies. Or a beautiful sunset. Or even a really nice letter.

It doesn't.

It starts with a Jupiter-size spitball stuck to the cafeteria floor, the one that was flung at the back of Graham Parker's head. He never saw it coming. But I did.

The school day is over. Almost all the students are gone. So it's the perfect time to hide the evidence.

On my toes, I peek through the tall glass windows that line the cafeteria.

All clear.

I pull the lever on the Mastercraft 300, and it glides across the floor like an Olympic ice skater.

"It's got a one-point-two-horsepower motor," Frances explains. She chews on sunflower seeds, carefully spitting the shells into a cup as she leans against the stage.

Custodian. Janitor. Whatever you want to call her, Frances is a floor-buffing wizard, close to retirement, and possibly my favorite human. She also has a deep fondness for sunflower seeds, which makes getting her a birthday gift each year pretty simple. And out of all of us kids who have to wait after school, I am the only one she lets behind the handlebars of this buffer.

To be honest, there is only one reason why Frances gives me the honor of waxing the floor with this fine machine.

My mother.

The principal.

I will not sugarcoat this. I will not pretend that it is fine. That never getting the chance to ride home on a bouncy school bus is fine. That staying after school until it gets dark is fine. That having virtually every kid at school scared of your mom is fine.

Because it isn't.

It is the worst.

Mom's fun side disappeared when she stopped teaching and was named principal, and now her serious side is her all-the-time side. But at least I get to use this floor buffer.

It's good to have connections. Sometimes.

"Cross back and forth horizontally, like you're mowing a lawn," Frances calls out.

I nod like I know what she means.

I don't.

"Overlap your lines!" she hollers. "And hover over the tougher spots!"

I overlap. I hover. I do whatever Frances asks me to do. Floor buffing day is my favorite. And now I have a purpose.

This cafeteria floor will be spitball free, and it will no longer be a reminder—to Graham and to everyone—that he is a kid who doesn't belong.

Except, even with the spitballs, the mean words, the laughter—Graham never flinches. It's as if he's covered with invisible armor and nothing can penetrate.

Confession: Even though he's the number one nobody at school, Graham Parker is one fascinating boy.

Here Comes Graham

When Frances heads out to replenish her sun-flower seeds, I run to my backpack and whip out a bookmark. A stiff bookmark is perfect for holding the spot in your book *and* scraping spitballs off the floor. Not many people know that.

Back behind the floor buffer, I channel my inner Frances. I overlap, I hover, I pretend to mow a lawn. "Take *that,* Joel Webber," I whisper.

Joel Webber.

He's the reason why I have to clean up this mess. What does he have against Graham anyway?

That guy should be knocked down a few pegs. He is friendly with all the girls, has a high-five relationship with the guys, makes everybody laugh, and is a favorite of some of the teachers. But not all. Joel has a mean streak mixed with a nice streak. The second is aimed at whoever his favorite person happens to be that day. The first, well, isn't.

Sound complicated? It is.

I know this because two years ago, almost to the day, his nice streak was aimed directly at me. (Or maybe it was his mean streak. It can be hard to tell them apart.) A few of us were sitting on the grass next to the slide picking dandelions. Joel was plucking blades of grass and twisting them together into a loop, like a ring.

And then before I knew what was happening, Joel was kneeling by me, showing off his bright, perfect teeth. "Allie, you should marry me!"

Before I could answer, all the kids around us were pointing, giggling. My face turned hot. Joel Webber was making fun of me. I knew it. So I turned and ran away from him, and the laughter got even louder.

Joel Webber's mean streak may have been aimed at me that day. But now that we're in fifth grade, it's usually aimed at Graham Parker.

Time for this mean streak to end.

As I turn the floor buffer around to make one final pass at the spitball, I glance out the cafeteria window.

Oh, no.

Here comes Graham, sauntering down the hallway, headed toward the cafeteria — acting as if he doesn't have a care in the world. Acting as if the Joel Webber Spitball Ambush of 3.5 Hours Ago never happened.

He is not alone. At his side, reading from a list attached to her clipboard while waving her hands around, is Lexa Cruz. Fourth-grader. Daughter of the school counselor. Extremely organized. Super chatty.

Lexa is also known as the cruise director. She actually gave herself that nickname, since her last name is Cruz, and she's great at making lists and schedules and having fun — something she reminds us of on a daily basis.

I let go of the lever and stop the machine.

Don't let them see you, Allie.

"Thanks, Frances. Gotta run!"

Frances has come back with a fresh supply of sunflower seeds. She winks at me. "No more help?" She gently pokes me on the shoulder. "You're getting pretty good at it, Allie Kid."

That's what she calls me: Allie Kid.

I love it.

But here's a confession: I don't want Lexa and Graham to see me hanging out with Frances so much. True, they have to wait after school every day just like me. They have for years. But *I'm* the only one on a nickname basis with the janitor.

And here's another confession: I'm also friends with the cafeteria manager. And the librarian. And all the teachers (minus the computer teacher who is ultra grumpy and constantly complains about wrist pain).

Add all that up, and I'm sure it does *not* equal "the coolest kid at school." I'd settle for "the girl who is treated like everyone else because her mom is not the principal." That's too long a title, I know.

Maybe that's why becoming that normal kid feels so impossible.

Pyramids and Pentagons

To be clear, I have no desire to be at the top of the School Coolness Pyramid—if that even exists. I'd be perfect as the base of the pyramid, or even a plain old boring side. Basically, I just want to be a *part* of something.

Specifically, I want to be a part of the Pentagon.

No, not the highly secretive government building near Washington, D.C., where military stuff happens. I'm talking about the Pentagon of Mountain Crest Elementary.

Some schools have great volleyball teams. Great basketball players. Or great spellers. We have a math club. One that has taken first place in the math Olympiad four years in a row. On the day of the competition, the Pentagon wears matching shirts, and the whole school gives them high-fives, thumbs-ups, pats on the back, first in line—all that. Each of the upper grades has an elite group of five members. They are rock stars here.

This year, if our school wins, it will be a huge deal. That's because a pentagon has *five* sides, there are *five* team members from the *fifth* grade, and this will be win number *five*. So everyone's freaking out.

Every school year, it all starts over, and anyone has a chance to become part of the Pentagon. The math teacher, Mr. Vicario, has announced the captain. It wasn't a shocker, since she has the highest math grade in our class. She always has, and she's always part of the Pentagon. But the remaining four people will be selected soon. Mr. Vicario will look at our recent test scores and decide who gets invitations. If there is a tie, the captain helps pick the members.

Since the beginning of the school year, I've been

practicing my math facts. I've been multiplying every number and fraction I could get my hands on. Whenever Dad goes to the grocery store, I go with him to estimate the cost and calculate the tax. "My little math maniac!" Dad calls me.

I like math and all, but that's not really why I want this. The truth is, if I'm chosen for the Pentagon, I'll be dripping in respect.

Almost everyone avoids me now like I'm some sort of rat — who tells on people and uses her connections to get them in trouble. (See: all previous info about my mother being the principal.)

There was only one time I was a rat. One time that I talked to Mom about something I shouldn't have.

ONE. TIME.

But some people won't forget it. It was last year, and only one person got in trouble.

True, the person was Chloe Alvarez. My former best friend. But I will forever regret telling Mom. If I'd just kept my mouth shut, maybe I'd still have a seminormal life.

And maybe Chloe and I would still be friends —something I want more than anything. The problem is, she went and made other friends.

But that's not the only problem.

The recently named captain of the Pentagon and the student who will help select the remaining members?

Chloe Alvarez.

The girl who refuses to talk to me ever again.

Sprite Deficient

I sneak out of the cafeteria and hustle up to Lexa and Graham before they can see where I came from. They're both drinking Sprites they got from the vending machine in the teachers' lounge. Since it's 3:45, Mr. Dancy, the PE teacher, was just in there finishing his lesson plans. I know this because Mr. Dancy finishes his plans every day by 3:45, like clockwork. He is also very generous with us after-school kids when it comes to our Sprite needs. Telling him we have a disease —Severe Sprite Deficiency!—always gets him laughing and emptying the change out of his pocket.

Lexa takes a sip from her can. "Where'd you come from?"

I'm breathing hard. "Down by the . . . you know . . . by the . . . thing—"

She doesn't wait for my explanation-that-really-isn't-an-explanation. "The meeting starts in five minutes," she says. "Band room. Be there."

Graham waves his clarinet case at me. "I'm in charge of the entertainment portion of the meeting."

I nod. "As always."

"Four and a half minutes," Lexa barks over her shoulder as she power-walks down the hallway.

"I memorized 'The Star-Spangled Banner,'" Graham says. Then he shoots me a sneaky smile, adds, "But I'm going to play it in double time for fun," and walks into a pole. "You okay?" he asks the pole, then laughs and heads down the hall.

There's so much to say about that strange boy, I don't know where to start.

I'll Start Here

His mom is a fourth grade teacher at our school. Our moms have worked together as teachers forever, and so Graham and I have known each other forever too. Honestly, I can't even remember the first time I officially met him — he's just always been in my life, like a cousin.

Except he's not a cousin.

I'm not sure exactly what to call him.

Usually you will find Graham with a drawing notebook in one hand and his clarinet in the other. But he doesn't play a rental clarinet you get from the school, the kind in a hard black plastic case lined with fake royal blue velvet. No, Graham's clarinet was handed down to him by his grandfather, who was in a jazz band—a *real* band that toured nightclubs and casinos and even played for the governor's birthday once. The case is made of worn brown leather, and the velvet inside is different. It's red, and it's *real*. Sometimes, without warning, Graham will whip out his clarinet and play a song and claim he can't help it because he is part jazz band player. His DNA, he says.

Graham wasn't always considered the weirdest kid in school. In fact, he used to be one of the most popular. But that was back during his ITCP: Intense Trading Card Phase.

Until it went bad.

All the kids used to bring Mammal-Morph cards to school—the ones where you collect mammals with superpowers and you combine them to morph them into more powerful creatures. Silly, I know. But, honestly, it was so much fun. At recess, kids would sit on the grass trading them. It became an obsession. Graham was the leader, because his collection of cards was legendary. He always had the rarest, the strongest.

Then when he started drawing his own cards and trading those, things really got crazy. His most popular one was a half mouse, half lizard named El Guapo—the flying superhero with a heart of gold and great hair. His superhero outfit was covered in exclamation points. Everybody wanted that one. For a while, all the kids put random exclamation points in their class work, and the teacher had no idea why. We would all snicker, and someone would say, "Beware the mark of El Guapo!" It was a whole thing.

The group of kids trading Graham's hand-drawn cards at recess grew bigger and bigger. Practically every kid in our grade was there, including me and Chloe. Chloe really wanted El Guapo, but I wanted Graham to make a special card for me.

"It could be half owl, half something else!" My owl fascination is a well-documented fact. More on that soon.

"Owls aren't all that powerful," Graham said.

I tried to change his mind. "They are when they shoot rainbow lasers out of their wings." But he never made me one. Too busy being the king of recess, I guess. But it was sort of nice to see Graham happy all the time.

As the crowd grew, some of the kids lost cards or thought somebody stole theirs. There were arguments. The arguments got louder and longer, and spilled over into class. There were tears. And the teachers got frustrated.

It was a Friday afternoon when Mom made the announcement. "All trading cards are banned at school."

Graham's reign was over. And kids weren't exactly clamoring to be friends with me, the principal's kid.

Graham still went to the grass every day at recess. But no one ever joined him. They moved on. Including me. Including Chloe. By then, everyone thought the cards were pretty stupid.

ITCP was done.

But not for Graham. Sometimes he would still talk about El Guapo and everyone would laugh. Mean laughing. So he stopped talking about him.

And that was the same time he stopped talking to me during school, too.

"If they laugh at me, they'll laugh at you." That was his explanation for ignoring me during the entire school day.

After school is a different story. Then he's old Graham. Happy Graham. He still talks to me about *The Epic Adventures of El Guapo!* That's the title of the comic book he's now writing.

I am the only one who knows this.

Part of me is honored to know his secret. But part of me wishes I didn't. Every day at recess he goes to the grassy patch with his drawing notebook. He scribbles and draws in it, working out the next scene in his book. But if anyone knew that he was still obsessing over El Guapo, they'd tease him forever.

Over and over I've told him to keep that notebook at home. That he should try to hang out with the other kids at recess. But every time, he responds the same way.

He flashes me a sneaky grin.

Looks left, then right.

Slyly, he whispers in a gruff voice, "What would El Guapo do?"

I roll my eyes and respond with the only answer he wants to hear. "Be epic."

To be honest, I'm still waiting for the day he makes me my own special trading card. But that day probably won't come.

The Principal Wears Fabulous Shoes

The sound always comes first.

Click-clack, click-clack.

Mom's high heels echo as she walks down a hall—you could hear her coming from another continent.

"Mom!" I call out. "Wait up." Since there are a couple of minutes before Lexa starts our meeting in the band room, it's the perfect time to ask Mom a favor.

I rush up to her, but she keeps moving. "Walk with me," she says.

We do a walk-and-talk. We do this a lot.

"Can we leave a little early?" I clasp my hands

together. "I really want some time to jump on Donny's trampoline before dinner."

Come on, Allie. You can do better.

I bat my eyes, flash a smile, the whole thing. "It gets dark soon—"

"I'll try." She cuts me off before I can even get to the good part. That I'm very, very close to completing a backflip on Donny's trampoline next door. The whopperflip with cheese, I call it. I'm not sure why it has cheese on it other than the fact that everything is better with cheese. That's a scientific fact. (I hope.)

Mom isn't interested in hearing about my whopperflip, cheese or not. "It's a busy day, Allie. Like I said, I'll try." She *click-clack*s off down the hall.

At least Mom is predictable.

Whenever she says *I'll try,* it means *impossible.*

As she rounds the corner and the sound of her *click-clack* heels disappears, I glance at the clock on the wall. The meeting starts in seventy-two seconds. Oh, boy—gotta go.

I head off down the hall, knowing I'll get there

in plenty of time. This school is an intricate maze —but I know all the shortcuts.

Confession: I also know where Frances stores the extra toilet paper, and I'm embarrassed that I'm a little proud of that.

For the Curious

To get from the cafeteria all the way to the band room in seventy-two-ish seconds, follow these steps:

1. You head down the sixth grade hall. I have no idea if this is north or south or what. Just get to the hall with one of those motivational posters. It either says BELIEVE IN YOUR-SELF! or READING TAKES YOU TO NEW WORLDS! It has a rainbow on it.
2. Turn right at the rainbow poster and take your first left.

3. This is the side entrance to the library.

4. Walk behind Mr. Landry's desk and go through the door that says WORKROOM.

5. On the other end of that room is *another* door, which leads to the teacher supply room.

6. Hurry through the supply room, because you're really not supposed to be there. (But be sure to give a quick wave to Mrs. Martinez, who is always laminating student artwork and never seems to mind when nonteachers cut through. She's cool, it's cool, keep going.)

7. Then head through the door on the other end, take a right and an immediate left, and that's where you'll find the band room.

8. Hello. You have arrived at your destination.

The Afters

I rush into the band room, short of breath but still on time. With me now in attendance, there are four of us. We are the Afters.

Lexa Cruz: fourth-grader, obsessed with horse books and "being in charge," currently sitting on the teacher's stool.

Graham Parker: fifth-grader, rarely seen without his grandfather's clarinet, currently sitting on top of an overturned trashcan.

Maddie Vicario: second-grader, very opinionated and very fidgety, currently spinning in the middle of the room.

Me, Allie West: fifth-grader, obsessed with owls, often dreams of having an ordinary mom who does little more at school than help with the book fair, currently the only one sitting in a normal chair like a normal human.

Because our parents work at the school, we all have to wait until they're done before we can go home. Most days we meet here in the band room, since Mr. Chapelle always leaves exactly nine minutes after school ends to rush over to the middle school to lead their after-school band practice. His room is always empty and unlocked, and the Afters know that Frances won't come in to clean until at least 4:15. Plenty of time to hold a meeting.

Lexa leads us. She always does and always will. These are words she actually said to us once. Technically, it would've made more sense for me or Graham to be the leader since we're both fifth-graders. But Lexa's posture makes you think she's at least a year older than we are, maybe two.

No one argued with her about being leader, so *bam*. Here we are, a group of Afters with Stand-Up-Tall Lexa as our cruise director.

Since our school is pretty small, there is no after-school program for all the kids who need someplace to go until their parents get home. Instead, they are bused over to the larger elementary school and join the YMCA class. So when the last bell rings, Mountain Crest Elementary clears out completely, minus the staff. And the four of us.

The Afters don't have much in common, but we're stuck with each other. So we make the best of it.

Repeat After Me

We're running short on time today, since Maddie needs to get to her gymnastics class," Lexa explains as she glances down at a list attached to her clipboard. "So let's plan ahead for tomorrow's activity."

I must say, Lexa does have good leadership qualities. She was born with a clipboard in her hand.

"Last week," she continues, "we cleaned out Mrs. Downing's truck and earned five dollars plus the coins we found in her glove compartment, which gave us $1.78 each. Thanks to Graham for helping us with the math on that."

Graham shrugs as he stuffs a cloth inside the

end of his clarinet, cleaning it for probably the tenth time today. He is always cleaning that thing. And he's always solving math problems with ease.

Not just math. He can recite historical events like they're letters in the alphabet. He can conjugate any Spanish verb without pausing. And he can divide fractions.

But he can't seem to figure out the simplest things: That clarinets don't need ten cleanings a day. That pants become too short when you grow. (You should quit wearing them.) That a pole doesn't need an apology when you bump into it.

And that guys like Joel Webber will fling monster-size spitballs at the back of your head if you do stuff like that.

Lexa continues with her list. "There are a couple of other options. We could go clean Mrs. Jensen's boards and try for some gummy bears. I heard from Allison Walker, who has a sister in her class, that they did a science experiment today involving gummy bears. So you *know* there are leftovers."

Maddie pouts, arms crossed. "Yuck. We clean boards for chocolate, or I'm not going." She keeps pulling her arms in tight, trying to get her fingertips to touch behind her back. She is the most opinionated second-grader I've ever met. And the most flexible.

"Oooookay." Lexa chews on the end of her pencil as she thinks. "I guess we could beg Mr. Landry to let us watch a movie in the library. But last time he shooed us out of there in a hurry because of a faculty meeting. So there's always the option of Eavesdropping Bingo."

I love Eavesdropping Bingo. We split up into two teams and listen in on teacher conversations, hoping to overhear the phrases or words we have on the bingo cards Lexa makes up. For example, if we hear "standardized testing," we mark that square with an *X*. The goal is to get four across, up, down, or diagonally. Last time, Graham and I won when we overheard the PE teacher say "darn it!"

It should be noted that if a team overhears an adult say a swearword worse than *darn it*, it's an automatic win. So far none of us has earned an automatic win.

"Let's take a vote." Lexa stands up and gives us a serious look. "We'll do this democratically — majority wins."

"Technically," Graham interrupts, "it's possible we won't get a majority of votes since there is an even number of people."

"I'm not voting," Lexa replies. "A good leader does what her team members are passionate about."

This makes me giggle. "Reading your mom's counseling books again?"

Lexa winks. "I'm up to the chapter called 'Dynamic Group Therapy.' Fascinating stuff."

Unlike the rest of us, Lexa intends to follow in her mom's footsteps and become a school counselor. Graham wants to become a jazz musician and travel the world. Little Maddie intends to become a famous ballerina and owner of America's largest cotton candy factory.

And me? All I know is I do *not* want to become a principal. Though I secretly want to wear high heels that *click-clack* while I'm walking down halls.

"Time to vote," Lexa barks. "Raise your hand if you want to do Eavesdropping Bingo tomorrow."

All hands go up.

"Bingo it is. Let's meet here right after school so we can get started early." Lexa waves us in to get closer. "Hands in. Repeat after me. We, the Afters . . ."

She stops and glances around at us; we're barely paying attention.

Lexa plants a hand on her hip. "Hands. IN!" She sighs. "You guys. It's important to say our pledge. Are you listening?"

"Hey! You stepped on my toes!" Graham says.

"I'll stop when you repeat after me." Lexa waits patiently, like all good cruise directors. She's the one who wrote the oath, of course, but we all say it. We stack our hands properly, stand at attention, and repeat after her:

> We, the Afters, will always try to better humankind.

We will be honest. And we will be loyal to each
other.
Our solemn oath is to keep our meetings secret
and sacred.
And whenever possible, we will bring snacks to
share.

When we finish reciting the pledge, Maddie closes her eyes and dips her head. Softly she says, "Amen."

Our Eight-Step Process
for Exiting the Building

It is 5:45 p.m. and time to go home. Let me give you the details of how the principal's kid leaves the building. This is how it is today, but most days are pretty similar.

1. I meet Mom in her office. She is standing behind a large table, moving some index cards around. It's her "plan of action" for how to get all grades in and out of the cafeteria for tomorrow's assembly by 11:30 a.m., when the kindergarteners show up for lunch.

2. Mom glances at the clock and says,

"It's late. Shoot!" No joke, she says this every day.

3. I throw away all the empty wrappers from the creamer and sugar she's been putting in her all-day coffee cup. That's right. Coffee. All day. Mom darts around the office gathering up everything she needs to work on at home.

4. We meet in the front office. Looking through the front windows, I can see that our car is the only one left in the parking lot. We are the last ones to leave. Even after Frances. As usual.

5. We start the drill: Mom flips off all the lights in the office, then puts her hand on the alarm box, takes a quick breath, and nods at me. That's my cue to dash to the front door and prop it open so she can get through it with all her belongings in under fifteen seconds. Any longer, and

the alarm goes off and the cops are automatically called. (That has happened to us twice.) But today we are on top of our game. We're both out the door in less than ten. As we head to the car, I see the first hint of a smile on Mom's face.

6. It's my favorite time of day.
7. But this is yet another late exit day.
8. There will be no whopperflip with cheese on Donny's trampoline.

Chicken Wings and Ducks

There you are! The game's about to start!"
Dad is already in his #23 jersey, buzzing around
in a frenzy as he sets out dinner. Hot sauce drips
down his chin as he polishes off a chicken wing.
"Do you want mild again? Or spicy?"

"Mild," I say. "Always mild."

I grab my paper plate and start the routine.

TV trays.

Coke.

Paper towels for napkins.

It's the off-season, but we have tons of basketball games recorded. Strangely, Dad rushes
around at the last minute like the game's about to

start and we *must panic,* because that's the art of watching basketball, he says.

This is our Monday night tradition.

We always order wings from Buffalo's Grill since it's buy-one-get-one-free night, buzz around in a hurry, and then at the last moment flop down on the couch to settle in for two hours of watching LeBron James stuff a basketball into a hoop. We don't even care that it's an old game.

Mom's role in this tradition is to take a bath, then afterward, pop in to snag a chicken wing now and then.

Dad used to watch basketball at the time it actually aired, back when he worked in an office where they made him wear a tic and be on time. Now he carves wooden ducks. He carves other animals too—bears, turtles, whales—but the duck is his signature product. Those are words he says when he's on the phone with people, usually while still wearing his pajamas.

He's following his dream, and Mom is the one with the big job now.

We can't even eat in the kitchen anymore, because the table is covered with his tools, wood glue, and scrap parts. Our shed out back — the one he adorably refers to as a "studio" — has been taken over by sanders, drills, wood shavings, and posters with inspirational basketball quotes.

A few times a year, Dad attends craft fairs to show and sell his carvings. In the weeks leading up to a festival, the house gets even more crowded with wooden animals and tools stored everywhere — on closet shelves, lamp tables, the top of the refrigerator. His happiness in those chaotic days leading up to the fair even seems to affect Mom; she smiles and kisses him on the forehead every time he whistles his cute little "the fair is coming" song.

Secretly, I've come to love the smell of fresh wood shavings.

"And LeBron sinks another three-pointer!" Dad announces. Usually, he fast-forwards through the commercials, but whenever it's getting late in the game and he's certain LeBron's team will win, he doesn't fast-forward. Instead, he turns to me.

"Tell me something. Something cool. Some-

thing awful. Your choice which comes first."
He says this every time, and it feels like a ritual
between us that will forever be the same.

Chicken wings.

Basketball.

Something cool/something awful.

Pulling my knees in, I hug them close as I
wiggle deeper into the couch. "First, something
awful. It's the story of a spitball."

His eyes grow big. "Wet? Dripping? Milk-
soaked? Details, Allie!"

It's hard not to smile. "Settle down, settle
down. I didn't get it analyzed in a lab. I just saw it
launch across the room, and from my viewpoint,
it was approximately the size of Jupiter."

"That's pretty small. What's wrong with your
lame classmates?"

I ignore his goofiness and continue. "It hit
the floor and dried there, so after school, I used
Frances's floor buffer to get it up. That and a
bookmark."

He gives me a knowing nod. "Who was the
victim? A kid? A teacher? Mom?"

"Not Mom. She would've already ranted to you and taken an extra-long bath."

"Soooo . . . who was the victim? And who was the criminal?"

I pause, listening for Mom's footsteps. Ratting someone out, even if it's Joel Webber, is not something I will ever do again.

In a low voice, I say, "I can tell you the victim. It was Graham."

"Your friend?"

"Yes. I mean no. He's not really a friend anymore."

"Oh, come on. You've known him since you were as tall as a yardstick."

"I'm serious, Dad. It's different now. We don't talk during school, only after."

"Then why are you cleaning up spitballs for him?"

This makes me pause. It's a simple question. Why does the answer seem so complicated?

Dad narrows his eyes, waiting for an answer. As much as I don't want to talk to him about that, I sort of like that he pries into my friendships.

42

He knows why Chloe stopped talking to me. He hasn't helped me solve that one, but he still snoops. Yet he's wrong about Graham. Right, but wrong. "Can we just watch the end of the game?"

He lifts the remote control high in the air, taunting me. "Not until you tell me something cool. I'm guessing you're not going to tell me much more about the something awful."

I search my brain. Something cool . . .

"They're going to announce who gets invited onto the math Olympiad team soon. I got an A on my last test, so I may have a chance to get an invitation. Graham helped me study."

He smiles. "Sounds like this friend-who-is-not-a-friend is the kind you should hang on to. Too bad he's getting spitballs thrown at him."

Suddenly, Mom appears at the door. When she's in slippers instead of high heels, it's like she's in stealth mode. "Spitballs? What happened?"

Time to zip it, Allie.

"Nothing, Mom."

I clam up. Dad clams up. We go all clamlike. Mom snatches a chicken wing and breaks the silence. "Set your alarm, Allie. We need to get to school early tomorrow."

Once Mom is gone, I grab the remote from Dad and hit Play. The crowd goes wild as LeBron slam-dunks the ball. "My guess is LeBron never had to go to school so early that it was still dark."

Dad thinks this over for a moment. "Never guess someone's backstory. You don't know the truth until you ask."

"Fine. I'll call LeBron and ask him about his childhood."

Dad nods. "Report back."

Confession: I don't actually call LeBron. His website only has links to his Twitter.

Call Me Sugar

My alarm goes off early. I groan, roll out of bed, quickly pull my hair into a side ponytail, get dressed, grab a banana, and fall into the car.

It's dark.

It's cold.

I forgot my jacket.

Mom and I walk into school at 7:10 in the morning, and the building smells weird. It *always* smells weird this early. The air has been off all night, and there's a staleness, like old bread. By the time the students start arriving, it'll be aired out and a bearable temperature. But in the meantime, my first hour of every morning is spent shivering.

The cafeteria. That's where I can find some warmth.

Frances is already in there, setting up chairs for an assembly. Just as she finishes a row, she looks up and spots me in the doorway. I attempt a little wave, but it's difficult since I'm rubbing my cold arms to get the circulation back.

Frances wags her finger at me. "Sugar! Where is your coat? You're freezing."

Allie Kid is the nickname she uses when she's feeling playful. She calls me Sugar when she feels sorry for me.

"Come on over—I got something to warm you right up." Without hesitation, she takes off her bulky sweater and hands it over.

"Thanks," I say.

The sweater is thick. It's huge. It smells like peanut butter. And it is fantastically warm. I'd snuggle in this sweater all day if I could.

"You can have what's inside, Sugar." Frances motions to the pocket.

It's a package of peanut butter crackers. That explains the smell. Yummy.

I sit on the stage and munch on crackers while Frances puts chairs in a row, then hollers back at me, "This one look straight?"

"Push the last chair forward. No, back. No, wait. Perfect." I dangle my feet and bang them against the stage. Between the two of us, we can get a room assembly-ready in no time.

Frances hasn't ever talked to me about retiring, but it could be coming soon. Recently, she's started wincing when she bends over. Back pain, I guess. She never complains, though. Frances is the definition of tough.

Her birthday is soon, and I want it to be a good one. Hopefully I can find barbecue sunflower seeds or *something* special for her.

Out the back windows I see the first bus pull up. My stomach sinks. It always sinks when I see the first one arrive. It marks the end of my secret life and the beginning of my not-so-great life.

I yank off Frances's sweater because there is no way I'd let any kid see that I spend my mornings wearing the janitor's clothes. "Thanks for the loaner, Frances!"

"No, no, Sugar. You keep it today. The weather girl, that one on channel five—oh, what's her name?" Frances taps her chin.

Kids are spilling out of the buses, headed for the door. I search my brain for the names of weather girls on channel five. "Mary Carpenter?"

"No, Sugar. She's that tall one with the eyes."

"Amelia Strong?"

Frances shakes her head. "Over at channel eleven now."

"Samantha Ferris!" I honestly can't believe I absorb so much information. Surely I can get a spot on the Pentagon.

"Yes, that's the one! Samantha Ferris said that today was going to be a chilly one. So go ahead, wear it." She motions to the sweater that I have already placed on a chair.

I glance at the buses. Kids are heading my way.

I glance at the sweater.

Buses.

Kids.

Sweater.

It's rude to turn someone down who offers you warmth and calls you Sugar.

But the choice becomes crystal clear when I see Joel Webber.

Don't Call Me Proud

I'm not proud of this, but suddenly I find myself fake-fanning my face. No way am I letting Joel make fun of me for being the weird kid in the janitor's sweater. "I'm already getting hot. But thanks, Frances. See you later!"

She winks. "Make it a good one, Sugar."

And now I feel bad. Why does being friends with the janitor have to feel like something to keep secret? Sometimes I wish I could cross my arms and say whatever I want without a filter, just like little Maddie.

Within moments, the halls are thick with conversation. Laughter. Screeches. Yelps. More laughter.

And finally, when most of the kids arrive, it fills with warmth.

Thank goodness.

Half of the fifth grade heads to the last two classrooms, and the other half heads to the first two, crossing paths and bumping into each other. Since we all move up to middle school before long, the upper grade teachers are slowly letting us get used to the idea of switching classes. Like a toe-dip instead of plunging in all at once.

So I spend half my day on one end of the hall until we swap classes after lunch. Next year, in the sixth grade, we will switch three times to get us ready for switching seven times in middle school. That's right — seven. Which sounds like a plunge into the very deep end of the pool.

For now, I will enjoy this toe-dip.

I clutch my books tightly as I dart between people, trying not to get shoved. But as I turn the corner, *Wham!*

Our foreheads bump. Books go flying.

I bend down to pick up the mess. On one of the books, I see a sticker.

My eyes drift up to meet hers. "I'm so sorry," I say softly. If only she knew I am sorry for *everything*.

Be calm, Allie. *Calm.*

Chloe grabs her belongings in a hurry and stands up straight. She takes a deep breath and she looks me over. "Allie—"

"Chloe! Birthday girl!" It's Andrea Fisher, interrupting our conversation—the one that was just about to become life-changing. Possibly. "Got your b-day invite in the mail yesterday." Andrea crinkles her nose. She always does this, whether she's happy or sad or smelling something icky.

Sofia Rossi joins us. "Got mine, too! I can't wait!" Sofia is the perkier one—if that's even possible.

Chloe nods and looks down. The weirdness of this moment must have hit her. That we're all suddenly standing together in the hall, the ex-friend and the new friends. That Andrea and Sofia just mentioned her birthday party. That her party is one I am not invited to.

Chloe's party is a different theme every year, and her mom goes all out. When we were younger, the entire class was invited. One year we all dressed as pirates. One year it was robots. Even Graham went. His robot costume was *the best* (and homemade, of course).

But then Chloe's parties started getting smaller. Friends, then just close friends. No themes, just hanging out at her house, eating and giggling, eating and giggling. I was invited to every single party—until now.

Without my brain's permission, my mouth opens and says the following: "I wish I'd been invited."

Why? Why do I let my mouth go out in public?

Chloe's eyes widen.

Andrea flaps her hands like she's panicking. "Gotta get to class on time!"

"Me too!" Sofia yelps, and then they both scurry away.

My stomach clenches, and I feel dizzy. If only there was something I could say to convince her that I want to fix this.

I nervously tug at my hair. "Chloe . . . um . . . I'm really . . ."

With a twirl, Chloe turns away and disappears into a sea of students.

Recess

There are only a few recess options for the upper grades. Foursquare. Basketball. Walking along the edges of the blacktop. Or wandering around the grassy patch.

No one chooses the grassy patch now that the trading card game is banned, even though it backs up to a beautiful field full of dandelions and honeysuckle bushes on the other side of the fence. The only person who goes out there is Graham.

When he's not drawing in his notebook, he makes musical instruments out of the stems of flowers and blades of grass.

Sometimes I want to join him. But he never asks. He never even looks my way. He just sketches in his book and wanders around making instruments out of nature. Nobody else does anything like that.

Today, I lean against the brick building, trying to come up with a sentence—*any* sentence—that will get me invited into the foursquare game a bunch of the girls are playing.

Chloe is waiting for her turn. This is it—the perfect time to stroll up to her and say something amazing. Something that will get her to talk to me, even if it's only about the weather. I figure if I keep putting myself out there, silence will turn to a sigh. A grimace will turn into a smirk. A nod will turn into a wave. A *hi* will turn into a sentence. And our sentences will turn into a conversation, one where I can finally say I'm sorry the way I want to, and we will find our way back to a friendship.

Deep breath, Allie. You got this.

I make my way toward my destiny.

Destiny, Interrupted

A face pops up in front of me.

"You're in a hurry. Where ya headed?"

It's Joel Webber, grinning, showing off his super-straight teeth.

I freeze. "Not headed in *your* direction, that's for sure."

"Technically you *are*, since you're facing me."

I spin around.

"So, this is rude, me having to talk to the back of your head."

Wait, he thinks *I'm* rude? I spin around again and face him. "What is your deal, Joel? Are you nice? Mean? What are you?"

"To the principal's kid . . . I'm nice." Through gritted teeth, he says, "I don't have a choice, right?"

"Do whatever you want." I lower my voice. "But stop launching spitballs at Graham Parker."

He throws his hands in the air like he's innocent. "I have bad aim! I was trying to hit the trashcan. Tell him to sit somewhere else."

"He should be able to sit wherever he wants without being ambushed."

"Wow. I'm impressed, Allie." Joel folds his arms and nods like he's got it all figured out. "You're going to make a good principal someday. Your mom will be so proud."

"Stop it."

"You can make up all the rules. That will be a blast for you."

"I don't make rules, and I don't want—"

"Except!" he interrupts. "You already have a rule—the one where you tell on people, especially your friends, and get them in trouble."

My heart races, chest tightens. I didn't mean to. And I'm not willing to give him the satisfaction of an explanation. Chloe is the only one who deserves to hear that. So I don't say another word, and I walk off.

Whack!

I don't walk fast enough, because Joel Webber beats me. He smiles and charms his way into the foursquare game. Within moments, he's made all the girls laugh. They think he's so cool. Funny. Cute.

"Throw it!" he says to Lainey Cooper. "As hard as you can!"

Lainey is the pitcher on her softball team. Throwing a ball hard is what she lives for. She flings it, and Joel puts his hands up, but not high enough. It whizzes by him, hurtling toward the grassy patch. Directly at Graham.

Oh, no.

Instinctively, I sprint toward the grass, my

heart pounding as I pump my arms, rushing to get over there. I don't quite make it.

Whack!

The ball hits him hard, knocking him to the ground.

"Aww, so sorry," Joel calls out.

Some kids giggle, but they try to hide it.

The yard duty teacher approaches Graham and pulls him up by the elbow. "Are you injured? Tell me what happened."

I freeze, not sure whether to say anything. Would he even *want* me to?

Graham wipes the dirt off his pants, then picks up the ball.

He glances at Joel.

Then at me.

"It was an accident," Graham says as he gently tosses the ball back toward Lainey.

The yard teacher seems to think everything's fine. She heads off in another direction, and the games continue like nothing happened. But I saw Joel reach for the ball. He knew exactly where it would go. He missed it *on purpose*.

My heart races. I want to run to Mom and tell on Joel. But I can't. I just . . . can't.

Graham gathers all his nature-made musical instruments scattered on the ground and stuffs them into his pocket, then tucks his notebook under his arm. With his head high, he marches off toward the school without looking back.

Just as I see Graham reach for the door, I notice something. Peeking out from the bottom of his shirt is some cloth — red cloth. My eyes drift up. More red peeks out of his collar. As I watch him disappear inside the building, I realize.

Under his clothes, Graham Parker is secretly wearing a cape.

Questions

Do I ask him about the cape?

What if he gets mad?

Or embarrassed?

Or, even worse, silent?

I see him in the hall. I want to ask him, but I don't.

I see him in math class. Again . . . want to ask . . . don't.

Every time the question comes to mind, the knot in my stomach twists harder.

I'm not sure why.

Maybe we all have secrets.

Lunch, Unfortunately

The **day crawls along as slowly as a fat cater-**
pillar. Every few minutes, I glance up at the clock.
The Afters will be holding our game of Eavesdropping Bingo. Since I will be Graham's partner,
I can hang out with him and not ask him about
the cape. I will not say a word. Not one word.

The clock reads 12:35.

It's time for lunch, unfortunately.

So here's how lunch works: Basically, everyone
dashes into the cafeteria like their hair is on fire
and tries to act like their hair is *not* on fire. It's a
delicate act of rushing around while simultane-
ously looking cool. This is not easy to pull off.

All the kids attempt to be the very first in

line for hot lunch. Well, not everyone. Some kids bring their own lunches, but usually only those with allergies or the picky eaters.

Personally, I am not a fan of lunch at school. Chaos and noise are not things I like to experience while digesting food. My only exception is Monday nights, when Dad and I watch basketball.

But I storm the cafeteria along with everyone else because of one thing and one thing only: half-frozen chocolate milk. The cafeteria manager, Ms. Jean, always puts the chocolate milk on the bottom of the box refrigerator, right under the regular white milk. She wants to try to make us drink the regular milk by making the chocolate milk hard to get.

But we're on to her.

The chocolate milk underneath gets colder than the rest. And if you can catch it on the right day under the right conditions, when you dig deep, deep, deeeeeep down in that refrigerator, you will pull out the most heavenly icy chocolate treat you can imagine.

There are only three people ahead of me in line. Today might be my lucky day.

Joel is first, like always. He doesn't get all hulk-like and mean in order to get to the front of the line. His approach is much more . . . stylish, I guess.

He always goes to the first person in line, tells them he is suffering from a certain horrible disease, and explains that this chocolate milk may be the only cure.

One time he had eyelid disease. One time it was rubbery bones. It's always something weird or wildly made-up, and everyone practically looks forward to letting him cut in line, just to hear what today's ailment will be.

"Pardon me!" Joel limps up to Ella Steiner, first in line. "My foot has gone numb, fair lady. The doctor says it's the worst case of pudding foot he's ever seen."

Ella smirks. "Pudding foot?"

"Yes, it's exactly how it sounds. My foot is full of pudding. Apparently, the only cure is extremely cold chocolate milk. May I?"

Ella bows. "Please, take my place. It would be my honor, Señor Pudding Foot."

Everyone laughs. I laugh too, but only a little.

We all peer in as Joel reaches deep into the refrigerator. "Touchdown!" he hollers as he lifts the chocolate milk high in the air and saunters back through the line. Life seems easy for him. He always gets what he wants.

Ella reaches in, digs around. "Oh, no. That was the last one!"

The rest of the line gasps.

Ms. Jean walks up to us, shaking her head. "Second-graders. They cleaned me out about a half hour ago."

My shoulders slump. The day was already awful. And now *this*.

At least there are Tater Tots.

View from a Corner Seat

After getting my food, I stake out my spot. Since I don't sit with Chloe at lunch anymore, I claim this corner seat every day so there's only one chair next to me that needs to be filled. Less rejection that way.

My corner seat is strategically located near the stage, where I have stuff to look at. There are posters on the wall, props from plays pushed to the sides, brooms left behind. This way I appear super busy looking at things, and I'm not super sad that I don't have a flock of friends by me.

I'm probably the only person in the room who puts this much thought into seating arrangements.

At least the Jennas usually sit at my table.

That's Jenna P. and Jenna R. They are very good at holding a lunch tray in one hand and a book in the other. These girls are readers. And when I say readers, I mean they read *all the time,* like even in the carpool line and even in the bathroom.

So of course they read at lunchtime too. Every few minutes, after flipping some pages, one of them says to the other, "What page are you on now?" They read like it's a competitive sport. It just stinks that they talk to me only when they need to settle an argument. Maybe they would talk to me like a human if I shared their reading habits. I love to read, but it's not like I'm trying to get into the Olympics.

"I really hope we're partners for the book project," Jenna P. says as she stuffs her mouth with a Tater Tot and flips a page.

Jenna R. nods. "Right? We would rock that report."

It's truly impressive how the Jennas eat, talk, and read all at the same time.

I lean forward. "What report?"

"I mean, we both read at virtually the same rate," Jenna R. continues, without answering my question. "It just makes sense for us to be partners."

I clear my throat. "What report?"

Both Jennas look up at me, almost startled. Their focus is amazing. Jenna R. laces her fingers together. "The book project with Ms. Santos. You get to do it with a partner."

"Which is super cool," Jenna P. adds.

"But Ms. Santos picks the partner."

Jenna P. pouts. "Which is super scary. What if I end up partnered with some random weirdo who doesn't speed-read?"

Reaching across the table to pat my hand, Jenna R. whispers to me, "Pray you don't get partnered up with a weirdo." She turns and motions to the other side of the room. Where Graham is sitting.

"He's no weirdo," I say, but it's a whisper and I'm not sure they hear me.

The bell rings. Like ants, the students file out of the room in an orderly yet chaotic rush. Before

I leave, I take a glance at Graham. I can't help myself.

I get a good view of the back of his shirt. Nothing—no red cloth.

The cape is gone.

The Possibility of the Perfect Partner

I soak in every word Ms. Santos says. Her instructions are simple. It's the details that have me bouncing in my seat.

"You will partner up and pick a novel to read."

Groans.

"You will work together in class. But you may have to finish outside of school."

More groans.

"You mean at each other's houses?" Joel asks.

"Possibly."

Louder groans this time.

Not from me. I'm excited. It's a struggle to sit still in my chair. What if Ms. Santos partners me with Chloe? She would *have* to talk to me; there'd be no way around it. I could say something about the project, then nonchalantly bring up the incident, tell her how guilty I feel, tell her how sorry I am, and *whammo!* Friendship restored.

"I want you to work together to create a three-D scene from the book."

Before all the groans completely take over the room, I raise my hand. "How do we choose which scene?"

"The scene where the main character changes the most."

Joel Webber shoots his hand up but doesn't wait until he's called. "You mean like an alien book? When they get infected and turn green—"

Ms. Santos shakes her head. "Emotionally, Joel." She pauses in front of his desk and taps on it. "When the character realizes he or she is wrong about something. And makes a change."

Again, I raise my hand. "Can we pick our partners? We'll be so productive if we pick them ourselves." I hope this suggestion will sway her to bend the rule for our class.

No such luck.

"I will choose the partners and announce them tomorrow."

Ugh. The odds of me getting paired up with Chloe are slim. This could be horrible.

But then I look over at Graham. His head is down, and he's not looking at anyone. Being partnered could be horrible for him too. Especially if it's Joel.

Graham could use some cheering up. It's a good thing the day is almost over. Time for Eavesdropping Bingo.

Holy Guacamole

In our long tradition of Eavesdropping Bingo, Graham and I are always partners. There is a reason.

Little Maddie convinced her dad, Mr. Vicario, to let her be with us older kids after school — like babysitters. Maddie promised him she'd always be with one of us, and we promised him we'd be responsible. That's how she joined the Afters.

So far so good.

But Maddie refuses to partner up with me or Graham. She says I walk too fast and she can't keep up. As for Graham: "He's goofy," she said right in front of him, because she does not have a filter.

"Thank you, Maddie," Graham replied, not sounding mad at all. "Goofy? I'll take it!"

So it's a given that Graham Parker is my partner in Eavesdropping Bingo. He always has been and always will be.

Lexa quickly writes out the bingo cards and hands them to us. "Check out the new phrases."

She's right. There are some new words on here.

Curriculum

Nightmare

Alphabetized incorrectly

Good grief

Holy guacamole!

Oh, this will be easy. If there's one person who will, without a doubt, mutter the phrase "Holy guacamole!" it's Mrs. Jensen, the first grade teacher. *My* first grade teacher.

"Follow me." I grab Graham by the elbow and drag him along, because he really has no choice. Figuring out which teacher will say which phrase is pretty much my area of expertise.

We head to the lower grades' wing, where everything is smaller and way more colorful.

"Shhh," I say to Graham as we pin our backs to the wall outside Mrs. Jensen's room.

Holy guacamole isn't the only reason we're here. I overheard Mom talking about some lesson changes for the teachers, and how some of them weren't too happy about it. I'm betting we might hear some talk from Mrs. Jensen that will get us more than one of our bingo words. She's really opinionated.

Peeking around the door frame, I see Mrs. Jensen pacing the floor as she talks to the other first grade teacher.

Squish.

Mrs. Jensen is wearing her chipmunk-brown sandals that make a wet-sponge sound with every step.

Squish.

"And how are we supposed to implement new curriculum when they keep giving us *more* new curriculum?"

Squish.

"It's ridiculous! Holy guacamole. What a nightmare."

Jackpot! Three bingo words already!

Down the hall, I hear the sound.

Click-clack.

Mom's heels.

I grab Graham's elbow. "Follow me. Time for a detour."

Finding Secret Spots Is My Jam

Right now I'm avoiding a walk-and-talk with Mom. What if she asks Graham about the incident with Joel at recess? What if she asks *me* how Graham got whacked by the ball? But that doesn't mean I can't spy on her afternoon meeting.

Pulling Graham by the elbow, I duck down a side hallway, cut through the counseling office, and push through the side door next to Mrs. Cruz's office (wave at her quickly) until we find ourselves right by the library.

We plop down on the floor next to the emergency exit. It's perfect because there are small windows in the library door, and when you're sitting down, the shadows hide you in the dark while you get a perfect side view of the meeting. Luckily, the librarian, Mr. Landry, seeks airflow today so the door is open partway. We can hear every word.

Graham pulls out his phone. I peer over his shoulder. "Whatcha doing?" I whisper.

He doesn't look up. "Using the timer. I'm timing."

"Timers are really helpful with that." I lean over to get a better look. "Aaaand you're timing what, exactly?"

"Her laughter."

That's when I hear it. The meeting hasn't started yet, and above all others, we can hear her.

Ms. Silk. Fourth grade teacher. She has this distinct laugh, a mixture of a howl and a snort and a cheer.

Woo-hoo-hoo-haa-haa.

It always goes on for longer than everyone else's. So then the people who stopped laughing start up again because Ms. Silk's laugh is so contagious. The room fills with infectious cackles. It sounds so fun it almost makes me want to become a teacher someday.

Ms. Silk is the teacher we all want. It's her laughter, her huge smiles, the way she calls everyone buddy. Graham and I both had her for fourth grade. (I won't lie and say I didn't beg Mom to put me in her class. I did. And Graham begged my mom, too. That's probably the only perk of being the principal's kid.)

I miss having Ms. Silk as a teacher, but not as much as Graham does. When I entered fifth grade and met Ms. Santos, it didn't take long for her to become my new favorite.

Ms. Santos is pretty strict, but for some reason, I like that she insists on having order in her room. It gives us a break from all the chaos. Gives *me* a break.

Everyone else is a little afraid of her, but it's not that way for me. I clicked with her on the second day of school when she was reading over my "What I Did This Summer" essay.

I wrote three long paragraphs about a fort I built near the creek in the woods behind our house. I shoveled a small cave out of the muddy hill using Mom's gardening tools. I created the roof with an old tarp. The seating areas were place-mats. And smushed into the mud walls were my RULES FOR THE CREEK CLUB. (1. Never tell anyone about the Creek Club. 2. Bring yummy snacks.)

Graham came over to my clubhouse once. But he said, "It's far too small and dirty, and the insects are murderous." Those were his exact words.

I never invited anyone else to my fort.

Sometimes I go for a hike through the woods and still see that hollowed-out part of the hill. The tarp is gone. Placemats gone. But it's still a good place to sit and listen to the creek. Even if you get muddy and murdered by mosquitoes, it's worth it.

Anyway. That's what I put in my three-paragraph summer essay.

Everyone else wrote about how much they liked Hawaii.

Ms. Santos asked me to come to her desk. She slid the paper over to me and pointed to the A-plus at the top. Then she put her hand on top of mine and whispered, "I'm impressed. I expect big things from you, Allie."

It was the whispering that made me a fan. The

fact that she wanted to keep it quiet, like it was a secret for just the two of us, made me realize that maybe—just maybe—I had something that set me apart.

Something more than just being "that girl who's the principal's kid."

Secrets Not Shared

Twelve seconds," Graham whispers. **"It's not a** record laugh, but it's pretty good. If anyone says the word *poop* or *duck,* she'll start laughing all over again. Hard consonants make her happy."

I poke him on the shoulder. "You know what would make me happy?"

"Being in charge of the world's largest owl museum."

"Yes, but I'm thinking of something else."

"Unlimited access to the soda machine!" He is a little too excited now.

"*Shhh.* Of course. But that's not what I'm thinking of."

He covers his mouth and talks out the side.

"You want to be picked for the Pentagon. You want to be friends with Chloe again."

"Well . . . yeah . . ." This is weird. I haven't even talked to him about Chloe. I cover my mouth too and whisper out the side. "How did you know that?"

"It's pretty obvious, Allie." He raises an eyebrow. "I saw you bump into her in the hall the other day, and you started talking. I'm sure that wasn't an accident."

I plant my hands on my hips. "It *was,* actually." Why would he think I planned that? Even though I totally would have if the thought had entered my mind.

"And then today you asked Ms. Santos to pick your own book project partner. I'm sure you weren't hoping to partner up with me."

Okay, he's right about this one. But the way he says it makes me sound like an awful person.

"Graham, it's not like I don't want to be your partner. You're the one who said we should never talk during school. Remember?"

His eye twitches, but he shrugs off the question

and snatches the bingo card from my hand. "We only need one more word. Let's just play."

We sit in silence. Waiting for a word. But they keep discussing the upcoming carnival fundraiser, and they are saying words like *baked goods* and *clown basketball.*

Graham bumps shoulders with me and says in a low voice, "So what was it?"

"It?"

"The thing that makes you happy. You never told me."

I take a deep breath, and say in a soft voice, "When a friend shares a secret."

"A secret."

"Yeah, a secret is something kept unknown by others."

"I know the definition, Allie West. The first book I ever read was the dictionary."

This makes me smile.

He shrugs. "Then ask me. What secret do you want to know?"

The cape, Allie. Ask him about the cape.

"Do you . . ." This feels wrong. So I say, "Why

doesn't it bother you that Joel Webber is mean to you?"

"He is?!"

"Shhh!"

"Sorry." He says this with a smile. "Look, the reason why his words don't bother me . . ." He pauses, then shakes his head. "Is because I have bad hearing. I can't hear a word the guy says."

"Be serious."

He cups his ear. "What?"

I reach out to throttle him, but he twists away and covers his mouth, trying not to laugh too loud.

Mom's voice booms over the group. "Now, let's talk about standardized testing."

Finally. I peer over his shoulder. That's it— four in a row. "We got it. Bingo! We're going to get so much candy!"

He stands and slings his backpack over his shoulder. "Keep it. I gotta go do some work."

We both know what he means by work. It's not homework, because he usually gets it all done before the end of the day. So any work he does after school is on his El Guapo comic book. At least he shared *that* secret with me.

He heads down the hall, bouncing on his toes.

"Be epic," I whisper.

Happy Graham, gone again.

Perks

I stop by the band room before heading to the office to wait for Mom to be done with her meeting. Maddie and Lexa are already there.

Maddie smacks her gum loudly as she waggles her paper in front of me. "We got *textbook*. That's it! I told Lexa to go to the gym, but nooooo—"

I wince as I hold up our bingo card, knowing it will make her even madder. "We got four —diagonally."

Lexa throws her hands in the air. "How do you two win *every* time?"

"We have secret spots. Remember, I'm here longer than you two every day. Having a horrible after-school life has its perks, I guess."

Lexa shoves her chunky glasses up her nose and narrows her eyes, trying to look menacing. She does not look menacing. Not with that grin creeping across her face. Even though she can be bossy, she's always seconds away from busting into all-out laughter. She has this raspy voice, and her laughs are almost as good as Ms. Silk's.

"You and Graham can have the candy tomorrow — no sooner!"

I don't think Lexa cares if she wins or loses. She just likes being the one to make up the rules.

"Where do we meet tomorrow, boss?" I ask.

"The stage in the cafeteria. I've come up with a great idea. It might possibly be my greatest one yet."

"Tomorrow. The stage. Your greatest idea yet. Got it, Director." I salute her, spin away, and head to the office. It's possible there's a bounce in my step.

The Afters are the best part of my day.

Ten Truths and One Lie

1. I know all the teachers' names.
2. What car they drive.
3. What they put in their coffee.
4. Where they keep their *good* pair of scissors.
5. Sometimes it feels like I am a member of a secret society.
6. When your mother becomes the school principal, they do not hand you a Cool card.
7. You are dealt the Reject card.
8. You are never invited.
9. Not lunch.

10. Not sleepovers.
11. Not birthday parties.

Confession: There is no lie here. It's all true.

Riding in Cars with Principals

It's one car. One principal. And it's virtually the same routine every day.

Mom moaning as she slips off her heels to drive.

"Oldies but goodies!" blasting on the radio at just enough volume that we don't talk.

The two of us zoning out during the ride home.

But today is unusual. My knees are bouncing. My palms are sweaty. It's about Graham, but not *exactly* about Graham.

He was right. I *have* to be partnered with Chloe. My life is all messed up because I confided in Mom last year. (Or ratted, according to some people.) So maybe — just maybe — I could confide in her again. But this time, it could fix everything.

All I need is for Mom to talk to Ms. Santos and ask her to choose Chloe as my partner. If having connections is part of my DNA, then maybe I should use them. I need all the help I can get.

So our normal zoning-out ride home suddenly changes. I reach forward and turn down the volume.

"Mom?"

She glances at me nervously. "Was I driving too fast? Sometimes I get lost in thought —"

"No. I just have a question."

"Something happen in school?" She grips the steering wheel like she's bracing for news. But telling on people is not what I do. Not anymore.

"Everything's fine. I just . . ." It's been so long since I've talked to her — *really* talked — that it feels weird. "It's about lit class."

"Oh. I heard you guys are working on a new book project."

"With a partner," I say.

Ask her the favor, Allie. Ask it!

"I'm sure you'll do great with whoever you get."

In a low voice, I say, "Chloe would be a good partner."

She pats my knee. "You guys still not talking? Surely she'll forgive you."

It's weird that she acts like she knows the details of my social life. I break down and share this ridiculous stuff only with Dad. Mom must be guessing.

"Not if I can't find a way to get her to talk to me."

"I could have a chat with her mother—"

"No! Mom, that would be so embarrassing."

Silence. We look at the road. We say nothing. It's awkward. Finally, Mom speaks. "You said you wanted to ask me a question—what was it?"

What I wanted was to ask her to nose her way into my business. To use her job to make Ms. Santos partner me with Chloe. This all suddenly feels so wrong.

Instead I say, "What book should I read for my project?"

She shrugs. "I haven't had time to read a book since last summer. I'm just too busy . . ." Her voice trails off, like she's daydreaming about summer vacation. And time to read.

"Never mind. I'll figure it out." I reach forward and turn up the radio.

Luck in the Air

For once, the class is silent. Ms. Santos stands at the front of the room, looking down at the list. This is it. I have dreaded this moment for the past 21.5 hours, ever since I chickened out from asking Mom for an insider favor. At this moment, I regret that decision.

"Lainey, your partner is Cassandra." They pull double fist-pumps because they're friends, and happily move across the room to sit together.

"Graham . . ."

Oh, no. What if she announces a name and the person groans? Or protests?

"Your partner is Jenna Paulsen." Jenna P. quietly gathers her books and sits next to Graham.

She doesn't moan or roll her eyes like she did yesterday at lunch. When she glances over at me, I shoot her a sweet smile to thank her for not being rude to Graham. I'm not sure she'll decode all that, but she nods at me.

"Allie . . ."

I swallow hard.

Not Joel. Please not Joel.

"Your partner is Chloe Alvarez."

I jump out of my seat. I can't believe it. "Chloe? Really?!" Some kids giggle.

Ms. Santos looks over her glasses. "Yes, Allie." She motions toward the open seat next to Chloe.

I slide into the chair and keep my eyes on my hands. As Ms. Santos goes through the rest of the partners, Chloe and I are silent.

For a moment, I savor the situation. Asking Mom for a favor wasn't even necessary. Good ol'-fashioned luck was on my side. It's such a relief that I didn't have to use my connections to set up this match. But Graham probably thinks I did.

When everyone is partnered up, Ms. Santos says, "Take several minutes to talk to your partner and decide which novel you'd like to read together."

Oh, no. What if I can't figure out what to talk about? Talk? For minutes? *Several* of them?! If I don't count yesterday, when Chloe said my name after I bumped into her in the hall, the two of us have not spoken in nine months, fourteen days, 4.5 hours. Roughly.

Partnering up with her suddenly feels overwhelming. I have no idea what to talk about. I open my mouth anyway and say . . .

Nothing. I say nothing. The words won't come.

"Um . . ." Chloe leans over her desk. "I remember that you like owls."

She is speaking to me. ME. I need to be calm, but ultra cool.

"Owls. Yes."

"Isn't there some owl series? Guardians of . . ."

"Guardians of Ga'hoole!"

She leans back, like my wave of excitement might drown her.

I lower my voice and clasp my hands together,

trying to display a smidgen of coolness. "It's a great series. I've read them all . . ."

"Oh." She looks disappointed.

"But it would be fun to start again at book one," I offer.

Chloe's face softens a little. "I'd like that."

"I have a copy at home, but I'm sure there's another one in the school library." I know this for sure because I'm the one who shelved it in the correct spot the other day, after school with Mr. Landry.

"I'll stop by there on my way to my bus," Chloe says. "How about we both read chapter one tonight?"

Jumping on my desk and squealing with delight would be too much. Instead, I calmly say, "Deal."

Strangeness in the Air

Lexa and Maddie are already sitting on the stage in the cafeteria with their legs dangling over the edge. That part's not strange. It's what is on their heads that's strange.

Lexa is wearing a tiara made of seashells.

Maddie is wearing a plastic coconut shell.

I toss my backpack to the side and hop onto the stage. "What's up with the tropical theme?"

The lights are on, and it's warm in the spotlight. There's something so magical about stage lights. They make you feel like something amazing is about to happen.

Maybe something amazing *is* about to happen.

"We all need hats for today's meeting." Lexa leads me back to the shadowy corridor offstage, where a wall of shelves is filled with props. "Ours are left over from the fourth grade production of *The Little Mermaid*."

"Why hats?" I ask.

She shrugs. "They're festive. And today is going to be a festive day. In fact, many more days are going to be festive." She gives me her signature sneaky-Lexa grin. "Trust me."

I search and search, then finally settle on a red genie's cap. The one the fourth-graders used in their *Aladdin* play.

Graham isn't here yet, but I know exactly which cap he will pick: the Tin Man's funnel hat from *The Wonderful Wizard of Oz*. It's his favorite play and movie and book. Yes, book. He is the only human I know who read that novel. Voluntarily.

The Tin Man is his favorite.

"Where is Gwaham?" Maddie sometimes stuffs candy in her mouth and then starts talking, and it's honestly very cute.

I pat her on the shoulder. "Gwaham is not here. I'll go find him."

There are only a few spots where I can be sure he might be.

1. The teachers' lounge, getting a Sprite from Mr. Dancy.
2. The library, in the science fiction section.
3. The dark hallway outside the library that leads to the emergency exit door.
4. His mom's classroom, working on his comic book.

The teachers' lounge is a bust. And the library is empty. So is the dark hallway. But hold up.

The exit door. It's slightly open, propped by Graham's backpack.

He's outside.

A Three-Point Surprise

I don't see him at first.

Then I look beyond the blacktop and the grassy field to the basketball court. There he is, shirt untucked, shooting three-pointers.

"Graham!" I march over to him. Out of breath. Holding the silver Tin Man's hat. "You're missing the meeting."

He ignores me. "This is for the championship, folks! Three, two, one, *swish!* He scores! The crowd goes wild!!"

This whole scene is unreal. Graham never plays basketball. All the guys play it at recess, but he either draws in his notebook or makes grass instruments. How did he just sink that three-pointer?

So I ask.

"How did you just sink that three-pointer?"

No answer, just another countdown. "This one is for the eastern regional championship! Three, two, one . . ."

Swish.

All net.

This is confusing. "Graham. You don't play basketball. How did you just do that?"

The basketball bounces away and rolls to a stop as he strolls over to me. Calm and relaxed. It's all very weird. We've known each other forever, and he is no athlete. Not to be mean, but I'm just stating facts here.

"My apartment building. It has a gym. So I go down there and shoot baskets."

"And you were going to tell me this deep dark secret *when?*" Why does he keep secrets from me?

He dodges the subject. "Allie, explain why you are currently wearing a genie cap while holding the Tin Man's hat. I mean, you've done peculiar things before, but this is right at the top."

I shove the funnel cap into his hand. "The Afters. We're meeting on the stage. With props. No idea why, of course, since Lexa is leading and she has some new great idea that will somehow be *festive*." I turn to head back. "You coming?"

"I kind of feel like shooting some more." But then he clenches a fist and his face sinks. It's almost as if the memory of Joel hitting him with a spitball and letting Lainey nail him with the foursquare ball has just caught up to him at tornado speed.

He shakes out his hands like he's letting his thoughts release out his fingertips. "My record is twelve in a row, and I want to break it today."

"But this idea Lexa has could be fun. And we could be partners."

"Imagine that . . ." He scoops up the basketball and shoots. "Being partners with someone without having to get your mom to set it up." *Swish.*

I knew it. He thinks I asked Mom to make Chloe my partner. "That was luck, Graham. I didn't say a word to Mom. And Chloe even said a few sentences to me. So, like I said, I'm lucky."

He rebounds and tucks the ball under his arm. "That's cool."

"Graham."

"I'm serious." The look on his face tells me he actually is. Which is nice.

And now this feels awkward. "Well, then . . . okay." I start back to the building. "Come on."

When I reach the door, I look back and see him still standing in the middle of the court, just looking up at the clouds, like he's counting them or trying to change their shape with his mind.

Then he sets the basketball down and kicks it over to the storage shed.

He heads toward the building.

I can't help but smile. He's wearing the Tin Man's hat, tipped just slightly to the right.

Confession: Stuffed under my bed is a copy of *The Wonderful Wizard of Oz*. I have read ten chapters and hope to finish it someday. Graham would like that.

Festive Indeed

The four of us sit in a circle on the stage wearing our stage prop hats.

Genie cap.

Tin Man's funnel.

Seashell tiara.

Coconut shell.

We, the Afters, are not the coolest cats in Catsville. (My apologies to any cats reading this who actually *are* from a town called Catsville. I'm sure you're super cool.)

I adjust the genie cap before it falls off my head. "I feel like a dork, Lexa."

"I'm crazy for coconuts!" Maddie says as she beams at us. I think anytime she gets to sit in a circle, crisscross applesauce, she feels in her natural habitat. Maybe the goofy hat is improving her mood even more. Maddie is having a moment, basically.

"What if we did this every day?" She gets that wild look in her eye. "And we act like they aren't on our heads, and when people look weird at us, we'll look weird back at them and then they'll wonder if *they* are crazy, and we'll realize the hats give us superpowers, and we'll solve mysteries and have our own theme music—"

Graham raises a hand. "I will be in charge of theme music."

Lexa seems unfazed by our lack of focus. "I have a plan—a big one." She pauses as she laces her fingers together, creating a dramatic moment. Her specialty. "Okay, so you know how the teachers have their holiday party? They secretly give each other a gift and then guess who the giver was and—"

Graham interrupts. "Secret Santa is the actual name of the gift exchange."

Lexa sighs. "Let me finish and then you won't

have to say all these things that aren't related to the positive prank idea."

Maddie tilts her head like a puppy. "What's a positive prank?"

Lexa sighs again. "And now I'm ahead of myself." She stands up, adjusts her seashell tiara, then struts out to the middle of the stage so the spotlight shines directly on her. Now it's all *very* dramatic. "We will each pick a teacher. Or the librarian. Or anyone on staff! Our job is to give them a secret gift, something they'd want, but not in an obvious way. Like, something that will just make their day, you know?"

"I've tried it once before," Graham says. "But sometimes the person doesn't know it's a gift. They don't know how much time and thought you put into it. They throw it away."

"Sheesh, Graham," I whisper to him. "Don't be such a downer."

"I'm a realist—there's a difference."

I poke him in the arm. "You and your obsession with words and their *actual* meaning."

He nods. "Weird, I know."

Lexa plows ahead, ignoring our banter. "For example, Mrs. Lee, the nurse, loooooooves strawberries. So I could bake a different strawberry dish for her every day of the week, then leave them in different places. On her desk chair, in her mailbox, on her car hood, wherever!" She throws her arms out and yells like she's addressing a real audience. "We're going to make this year count—really count!"

Positive prank.

Is it festive? Indeed.

Completely awesome? Yesssssss.

An Explanation

Mom did something like this for my birthday once; it became my birthday *week*.

I got an owl mug. Owl stationery. Owl night-light. Owl umbrella. Owl lunchbox. And an owl hoodie sweatshirt.

I inherited my deep respect for owls from my grandmother. Nana.

When I was little, we would sit at her kitchen table, and she would draw me an owl—any kind I wanted—and she'd write a caption underneath. It was always a piece of advice.

Never give up.

Time to soar.

Sure, I'm cute, but I'm smart.

Owls = awesomesauce

Awesomesauce. I always loved it when Nana said that word.

Ever since she died, I've kept the stack of drawings she gave me in a shoebox under my bed.

So there I was with six owl birthday presents, but the seventh was the most special. That was the day Mom turned to me and carefully laid something in my hands. "Nana wanted this to go to you when the time was right." She cupped my chin. "Now is the time."

I looked down and saw Nana's favorite necklace, the one with a mother owl nuzzling her baby. "For me?" My voice cracked.

"Owls represent wisdom," Mom explained. "And they are considered the keepers of secrets. They're special. Nana knew that about you, Allie."

I could not have missed Nana any more than at that moment. She was always encouraging me to be bold. Nudging me to do the right thing. *Time to soar!*

So every day from then until now, I have

carefully put on the necklace, and every night I carefully take it off. "Good night, Nana," I always say to the mama owl.

My grandma reminded me of the fun part of Mom.

I miss those owl presents. And I miss seeing Mom's fun side. She just doesn't have time to make my birthdays the most special week on earth anymore. Nowadays, it's as if Mom is covered in armor. Tough. Serious. Never going to break.

Lexa starts hopping around the stage with excitement. "We'll do stuff for the teachers that'll make them smile. Something unexpected. Something wonderful they'll never forget." More hopping.

"It's awesome," I say. And then an idea comes to me. I jump up to my feet. "Let's call the project Random Acts of Awesomesauce."

Maddie hops up and joins me and Lexa in the spotlight. "I'm in!"

I turn and squint at Graham. "You in?"

"Some clarification first," he says.

Maddie moans. "I don't even know what that word means, but I don't want any."

He pushes his way to the center of our circle and counts off his fingers. "Can we pick anyone we want? Can we give a service, not a gift? Can it be one big gift, not a bunch of tiny ones?"

"Doesn't matter," Lexa says. "Give your one amazing big gift to the person of your choice. Or give lots of little things to many people. This is supposed to be fun, Graham."

He stares off in the distance like the answer will appear in the air. I guess it does, because suddenly he says, "I'll do it."

When a Menu Is a Hat

Extra garlic rolls?"

Mom isn't paying attention. The cashier clears her throat and tries again. "Mrs. West. Extra garlic rolls, like usual?"

I nudge her. Mom startles. "Oh, yes! Garlic rolls. Extra. Yes."

She is the definition of distracted.

Picking up dinner on our way home was unexpected. Dad has a craft fair coming, so he's swamped with work and covered in sawdust. He's almost finished with his latest elephant project. That's why he didn't have time to buy groceries, and it's why we're standing in Provino's — my favorite Italian restaurant. The upside to Dad being swamped and covered is that I am the one who gets to choose the restaurant. Mom said she's so exhausted from making decisions during the day she can't possibly make one more.

Sooooo hello, Provino's. Your garlic rolls are a dream.

As we wait, I notice a family sitting in the restaurant; they're all laughing. The little girl is maybe two or three. She claps her hands. "Again! Again!" The mom takes her menu and folds it into a hat. Then she pretends it's a book. Then she pets it like a puppy. And then she says, "Oh, wait! It's just a menu!" The little girl howls with laughter. It's insanely cute.

"Did you ever play games like that with me?" I ask Mom.

She shrugs. "Peek-a-boo, I guess."

"I mean goofy games?"

"Sure I did." But she doesn't sound too convincing.

I change the subject. "So, Dad is pretty excited about the new elephant carving."

"Sounds like it." Mom presses her lips together. "Lucky guy."

"Lucky?"

Mom flattens out the wrinkles in her skirt as she explains. "He's in charge of his own time. In charge of his creativity. In charge of his job and nobody else's. He doesn't have to be in charge of everyone else."

For the first time, I realize that maybe she's a little jealous of Dad. He left his office job for a dream job. The transition wasn't even that difficult for him. Sometimes I think Dad takes a peek at those drawings under my bed: *Time to soar!*

Mom leans in closer to me. "Sometimes do you wish I was the kind of mom who would pretend a menu is a hat? I mean, now?"

My first thought is *yes*. She needs to let her goofy side come out. But at the same time, she *is* the principal. Being serious is probably a requirement.

Then a memory hits me. When I was in third grade and she was still a teacher, Mom's

Halloween costume was Marge from that TV show *The Simpsons*. The rule was you had to dress up as a fictional character, but not a scary one. For days, Mom plucked cotton through rolled-up chicken wire and then spray-painted it blue to make a tall wig. She painted Styrofoam balls red and strung them together to make a necklace. She even took me with her to the thrift store to buy an old green dress (and she bought me an owl pencil sharpener). Her costume was voted number one by all the students. Mom would talk to people in that raspy Marge voice, never breaking character. I think I hugged her three times that day.

But a few months later, she was promoted to principal. She never dressed up for Halloween again.

"Order up! Extra garlic rolls!" The cashier hands Mom several bags loaded with lasagna and spaghetti and dreamy garlic rolls.

"Let me help." I grab a couple of bags from Mom's hands.

We listen to the oldies music station on the drive home. We don't discuss her goofy side — or lack of one. I wish I *had* told her that I miss the mom who could go through the whole day in her crazy Halloween costume and never break character. If only the garlic rolls had arrived a few minutes later.

But then I realize: At least she asked me the question. She wanted to know if I miss the fun —if I miss *her*.

A tiny piece of Mom's armor got chipped off right there in Provino's.

I'll take it.

Counting Cans

It's early the next morning, and I'm filling out inventory charts with Ms. Jean in her storeroom. Really my job is just to count the spaghetti sauce cans and holler out the number. This really isn't much of a job. More like a blast.

Ms. Jean and I make a good team. She always seems to know the exact moment I've finished counting a stack. Our rhythm is impressive. Also, she is obsessed with Christmas and never takes down her decorations; the warm glow of the white twinkling lights that decorate her office makes me happy.

Ms. Jean is more than our cafeteria manager. She's a family friend. She used to stop by the house and pick up Mom to go on adventures together. But Ms. Jean hasn't been by in a while.

"How many?"

"Thirty-three!" I holler.

She scribbles that down in a rush. A large order arrived this morning, and she's scrambling to get it all organized. While she hauls in another box full of cans, I peek my head out the door to see if Frances is still moving cafeteria chairs. I like to look in and wave at her from time to time.

Except what I hear isn't Frances, but laughter and conversation. The students have already started trickling in. Oh, no. Oh, no!

Usually I leave early enough, before the beginning of class, so no one sees me working behind the scenes. Now it's late. I'm stuck in here. This is a disaster.

"Allie? Where are you, hon?"

If I'm quiet enough, maybe she won't find me hiding behind this door.

"What are you doing back there?"

She finds me.

"Are you hiding, Allie?"

I look at my feet. "Yes."

"That busload of kids just showed up. You're embarrassed to be seen in here working with me, aren't you?"

"Ms. Jean, I'm so sorry. I shouldn't—"

She squeezes my hand. "You don't have to be sorry. It's gotta be hard having your mom be the boss of everyone now. It's different for lots of people."

I look up at her. "You two were friends."

"Used to go to the gardening club meetings with her. And years ago, the two of us planted that tomato garden out back of the school. We even painted the boards for the raised beds." She winks at me. "The polka dots were her idea."

"Really?" This makes me smile. "But she doesn't work in the garden with you anymore, does she?"

"Look, hon . . ." Ms. Jean places her hands on my shoulders. "Your mom is a busy lady. I understand that now. But I sure do miss her."

Without thinking, I wrap my arms around her and whisper, "I miss her too."

She pulls away and gives me a reassuring smile. "I have an idea. Follow me."

Dragging me by the hand, she winds around the hallway beyond her office. Unbelievably, these are halls I've never seen before. She carefully pushes a door open and peeks out. "It's clear."

Ms. Jean motions to the girls' bathroom—the one near the library. "If you scoot across in a hurry, no one will see you."

"Ms. Jean. Thank you for—"

"Go!"

I sprint across without being spotted.

Whew!

In the bathroom, I take a minute to fluff my hair and wash my hands. But then I hear a toilet flush.

A girl walks out of the stall, and our eyes meet. It's Chloe.

Needed: One Miracle

She jumps a little when she sees me, then plays it cool. "Oh! Umm . . . hey."

"Hey," I say, also playing it cool. Then we eyeball each other for a moment. Which doesn't feel cool at all.

"Why are you in the bathroom way over here?" I ask. "Our class is in the other wing."

Chloe tugs at her braid, like she's nervous. "I forgot to stop by the library yesterday to pick up that owl book. I didn't want you to know. I figured I could grab it now and read the first chapter during lunch, but I promise I'll finish it—"

I hold my hands up. "It's fine. Really."

She looks at the floor. "You probably remember how weird I get when I miss a homework assignment."

The girl practically notifies the FBI if she can't find her homework. "Yeah. I remember."

Chloe has never gotten in trouble in her life. Except that once. Which is why it was such a big deal when *I* was the one who got her in trouble.

Chloe washes her hands and reaches for a paper towel. They're gone. She twirls around to face me. "You probably know where the new rolls are."

"Why would I know where to find the toilet paper?" My voice is a little sharp. Just because I'm the principal's kid, she assumes I can find bathroom supplies?

"Paper towels," she corrects me. "I wasn't trying to be mean. Just wondering if you could help."

And now I feel like a jerk for being, well, a jerk. "They're in the cabinet under the sink."

As I head out the door, Chloe calls after me. "Can I ask you a question?"

I prop the door open with my knee and turn back to her. "Sure."

"I want to get a head start on this book project. Would you mind working on it together after school at my house tomorrow?"

Whoa. Did she just say that?!

"Uh, sure." I say this super casually—even though my heart just did a celebratory backflip.

"You still remember where I live, right?"

I used to go over to her house practically every weekend, so of course I remember. "Over on Stonebridge, seventh house on the right." That probably sounded way too eager.

"The only time I can work on it is four o'clock. After that, we have to go to my brother's swim meet. Oh, wait. Your mom. I forgot—you always stay at school until late."

"It's okay. I can make it." Why did I just say that?

"You sure? We can probably get it done during class. You don't have to—"

"No!" I hold my hand out like a police officer stopping traffic. "I'll be at your house. Tomorrow.

Four o'clock." This could finally be my chance to tell her how sorry I am for last year. A chance to make this right with her. "I'll be there, promise."

"Cool."

She walks past me as I hold the door open. In my shock, I keep holding the door, not quite sure what to do. I just promised to be at her house at four o'clock.

Me. The principal's kid.

If it's not a medical emergency or a doctor's appointment planned four months in advance, Mom *never* leaves early.

I need a miracle.

Bathtub Talks

For normal kids, asking their mother to drive them to a friend's house is no big deal. But for my mom, it means changing her schedule and moving meetings and doing things that give her headaches.

Lately, it's even worse. Mom keeps murmuring about the upcoming school carnival, where we play games and eat funnel cakes and raise money for PE equipment. She's always rubbing her temples and using phrases like "so frustrating" and "taking up all my time."

So the odds of me getting a ride from her are slim. But with Dad nonstop in his studio, carving for the craft fair, he's a lost cause.

I have to give Mom a shot.

That evening, I wait for the perfect moment. The time when she is most relaxed, open to possibilities, humming her favorite song, and submerged in water.

I knock on the bathroom door. "Mom?"

She keeps humming. It's one of my favorite sounds, that combination of Mom singing and splashing. I pause to listen for just a moment more.

But now I need to get down to business. "Mom!"

"Yes? I'm in the tub."

"I know. Can I ask a quick question?"

"I'm in *the tub*."

"Right—I know. I can ask through the door. You don't need to move a muscle. But if you make splashy noises, that's fine. I can work around it."

I hear a little laugh. "Um, thank you. Ask away . . ."

I lean against the door and slide down to the floor. "It's about tomorrow. I need a favor."

All I hear are the drops trickling from the tub faucet.

"It's a pretty big favor. But it's important."

"Go ahead . . . ask."

Deep breath—here I go. "First, a little background. You know how Chloe and I haven't been talking since—"

"Since she got in trouble last year. She *still* won't talk to you?"

"Still. Or just when she has to, for school. We're not friends."

"Honestly, I don't see why she's blaming you. She's the one who broke the rule."

The problem was all about the trading cards. When Mom outlawed them at school, she sent letters to all the parents explaining the ban. Told them how the cards were disrupting the learning environment, blah, blah, blah. And her letter explained the consequences if any student brought the cards to school.

Three. Days. Detention.

Since Chloe was always such a rule follower, it surprised me that she brought that El Guapo trading card to school after the ban. It even surprised Mom.

"Mom, I have no idea why she brought it. We all know she's not usually a rule breaker. But maybe . . ." I pause, wondering why Mom and I have to talk about big things with a closed door between us. Maybe it's the only way. "I shouldn't have told on her."

I hear the water splash around, as though Mom has sat up. "Allie. If you hadn't told on her, other kids might have gotten the idea to sneak in their cards too. Rules are rules. You did the right thing."

How it all happened was just bad luck for me—bad luck that ruined my friendship with Chloe. Last year, we switched classes for math, so we swapped desks, and I was assigned to Chloe's. I liked to draw pictures and leave them for her there. I drew smiley faces, cats with sunglasses, and my favorite: stick figures diving into highly unusual liquids—lava, melted chocolate, tomato soup—anything I could think of to make her laugh.

But on the day I found the forbidden El Guapo trading card in her desk, I realized that my seat assignment was not such a great thing. Chloe would get in so much trouble if the teacher found that card.

So that's why I tried to stuff it into the back of her desk. But that was the exact moment that Mr. Vicario, my math teacher and Maddie's dad, stopped at my desk to hand me a worksheet.

"Allie?" His voice was deep and rattly.

I startled. "Yes?!"

The card flipped out of my grasp and fluttered to the floor.

"What is *that?*" His voice boomed. He snatched the card up off the ground. "A trading card? You know the rule, Allie. This is disappointing."

I was a disappointment to Mr. Vicario? This couldn't be happening. We had made big promises to him that we would take good care of Maddie after school. The Afters were responsible kids. Not *disappointments*. This was awful. I couldn't ruin little Maddie's time after school. She loved that small taste of freedom.

"It's not my trading card. This is Chloe's

desk!" I was thinking about little Maddie, but I didn't take a moment to consider what those two sentences would do to Chloe.

The entire class glared at me. Even Graham glared, like he couldn't believe his El Guapo card was suddenly the center of attention but for all the wrong reasons.

Mr. Vicario believed me, but he sent me to the office to tell Mom what happened. So yeah, I'm a rat. Chloe got detention for the first time in her existence, and I lost a friend. It was also the first time a teacher ever called her house with bad news. She was devastated. Her mom was livid.

Or so I'm told. It's not like she's ever talked to me about it.

Back to the bathtub. "Mom, Chloe and I got paired up for the book project."

She sighs. "I know."

"You do?" I don't even remember telling her.

There's a brief pause and a little splash. "It's a good thing, right? Maybe you can patch things up?"

"Yeah. It might give us a chance to finally talk."

"So what's your question, honey? The water's getting cold—I should get out."

"We're going to work on the report together after school tomorrow."

"Wonderful."

"So I need a ride to her house at four o'clock."

Silence. Not even a ripple in the water.

"Mom. Please." I press my head firmly against the door. "This is my chance to finally make this right."

I hear her flip the drain open and get out of the tub. Wrapped in a towel, she peeks out the door. "I'll have to rearrange some things."

"Really?" I jump to my feet.

"I'll try my hardest. I promise."

"Thank you, Mom. Thank you!!"

"Now, go to bed—we have to get there early in the morning."

"No problem!" I skip down the hall to my room, bounce onto my bed, and snuggle deep under my covers.

Confession: For the first time I can remember, early alarm and all, I'm actually excited about going to school.

Above It All

At lunch, I wave at Chloe. She glances at me while she's midconversation with Andrea. She doesn't wave back, but she doesn't look away, either. So on my way to my regular corner seat by the stage, I stop by her table.

"I can come to your house today. Mom's going to drop me off—which is sort of a miracle."

Andrea giggles.

Chloe glares at her. "Why are you laughing?"

"Because parents dropping off their kids is a pretty normal thing. Not exactly a miracle." She air-quotes *miracle*.

This makes me feel stupid. But then it hits me that my mom can't drive me everywhere because of her job. She's *the boss*. Which is pretty . . . boss.

"She's the *principal*," I say, matter-of-fact.

Andrea huffs. "It just sounded funny, that's all."

Chloe looks up at me, grinning. "See you at four."

I float over to my seat, feeling a little bit lighter. Chloe Alvarez practically defended me.

I spot Graham on the other side of the room and hope he'll look my way. This light, happy feeling is something I want to share. Maybe I'll sneak him a thumbs-up or a goofy smile. But he appears busy, in a corner chair at a table by himself. His lunch tray is full of chicken nuggets, and he's busy stacking them into a complex structure.

I wish I could fix this for him — this being an outsider. Graham has it so much worse than I do.

He used to be teased for his hair that was never combed and his pants that were always too short. Good ol' third grade meanness. But then the trading card obsession happened and suddenly Graham wasn't teased anymore. He was respected. But now that it's over, he has gone back to being told, "Scram, Graham!" Which is so dumb. Kids think they're being witty for simply rhyming two words.

As I head to my chair, I hear a commotion.

Joel Webber is pacing around his table of boys, all laughing. Something is in his hand, and it's not a spitball. This is entirely different. I can tell by the look on his face.

He looks around, then quiets his friends down, even though they're about to fall out of their seats trying to choke back their laughs. I follow Joel's line of sight. He's aiming at the trashcan.

What a weirdo. Why is it cool and funny to throw things across a room and try to make them land in cans? Did man evolve just to do this ridiculous act in school cafeterias? I hardly think we have opposable thumbs for *that*. I turn away and head straight for my regular table, where the Jennas are already speed-reading and speed-eating.

"Hey," I say.

No response. So I dig into my dessert first: blackberry cobbler. It was my begging that got Ms. Jean to order the cobbler. She was worried the kids wouldn't eat a dessert that wasn't chocolate and/or pudding. Turns out, everyone loves cobbler. It's my anonymous gift to this school.

My legacy.

It's possible I should have bigger goals.

As I ponder this idea, I hear a *SPLOOSH!* Then another. Then laughter.

I keep my eyes on my cobbler. Watching Joel Webber get attention for throwing something that makes a splooshy sound is not my idea of a good time. But then I hear whispers near me. Glancing around, I realize everybody's looking at me. *Me.*

"Isn't she going to tell?" I hear.

I scan the room. Looking at the mess on Joel's table, I can see they made a giant milkball. It never made it to its target—the milkball is now smushed on the floor next to the trashcan.

I hate that Frances will have to clean that up. And I hate that I'm probably the only one in this room who cares that Frances has to clean it up. After school, I always try to get to the spitballs before she does.

As much as I want Joel to get in trouble, I can't risk it. Telling on Chloe nearly ruined my life.

I can't be the snitch ever again.

Every kid in here is either laughing along with Joel or looking at me, wondering if I'm going to rat on him. Graham isn't doing either—even though he's sitting near the evidence, he doesn't even seem to notice. He just picks up another chicken nugget and continues with his structure.

Quietly, I go back to eating my cobbler and wait for the eyes to turn away from me.

They finally do.

At the end of lunch, I head toward the exit and see Graham up ahead of me. Some other boys cut in line and get behind him. They call out, "Scram, Graham!" But he just shrugs his shoulders and walks on, unflustered.

I want so badly to tap him on the shoulder and ask him how he does it. How does he make it through the day without letting them get to him?

Then my eyes drift down and I have my answer. Peeking out from under his shirt is red cloth. Again.

But as I get closer, I realize it's something more. The fabric has little blue exclamation points all over it. This is not just any red cape. Graham is wearing the cape of El Guapo.

!!!

The Final Bell

At the end of the day, I grab my books and rush to Mom's office. I can get my homework done there before we leave for Chloe's house. Also, if I'm in the office, I'll be right by Mom's side and she won't be able to forget. I don't even take a moment to stop by the cafeteria to tell the Afters I won't be at today's meeting.

"Mom! Mom?"

She's not at her desk.

"There was a bomb scare."

I whirl around and see Joel sitting at a desk facing the wall.

"What? A bomb?!"

He smirks. "Just kidding."

I realize I'm clutching my chest. "Don't do that to me." I have to lean against a chair to get my heartbeat back to normal.

"She left," Joel says. "Went roller skating."

"Very funny."

"No, wait—it was scuba diving."

"Stop."

"Actually, she went to solve a murder mystery with Scooby-Doo."

"Shut up."

Joel throws up his hands. "Wow. Principal's kid has a mean streak."

"Why are you in here?"

He points to his math book. "Doing homework. Also known as detention. There's no room in the dungeon, so the ogre put me in here. In that sentence, the ogre is your mom."

"So classy, Joel."

"Who, me? Nah. I'm just a commoner. No need to praise me. But if you must, go ahead and praise me all you want." He does a pretend wave to a crowd like he's their king. Joel certainly has an active imagination. I just wish he'd use it for good.

I cross my arms. "You're here because of the milkball at lunch, right?"

"I was just trying to throw it away. Don't blame me—blame my ungifted left arm."

There is no way I'm staying in here to listen to another crazy thing come out of his mouth.

"Awww, leaving so soon?" He gives a fake pouty face.

"I'm going to the dungeon." I close the door on him, pretty hard too. It feels good.

I flop onto the bench outside Mom's office. It's not all that comfortable, but I can get my work done right here with my papers on my lap.

Two worksheets later, I glance up at the clock. Oh, no—3:55.

And Mom's not here.

The Hunt

Where could she be? I hunt around the build-
ing, searching in all the usual spots: cafeteria,
library, the sixth grade hall. Sixth grade is always a
possibility, since there is some drama on an almost
daily basis. But the sixth grade wing is quiet.

I expand my search to every other wing. Along
the way, I pass a couple of teachers.

"Nope, haven't seen your mom, Allie."

"She must be here somewhere!"

No one has seen her.

Then I turn the corner to the fourth grade
wing and end up face-to-face with a mop. "Watch
where you're going, Allie Kid!" Frances says.

Oh, thank goodness. Frances! She will know

where Mom is—Frances is the brain of this building. And heart. And lungs. And wow, that got weird quick.

"Have you seen Mom?" I clamp down on Frances's arm. "She's driving me somewhere, and I'm late. I have to find her!"

She takes a long breath. "Sugar, she's down there, having a meeting." Frances points to the last classroom on the left.

Mrs. Parker's room.

Graham's mom.

"Sugar, don't—" Frances tries to stop me, but I take off anyway. Whatever Mom's talking about can wait.

As I near the door, I hear her voice. It's different. "Just tell the truth. Please."

Peeking in, I see Mom leaning over Graham. His face is red and splotchy. He's crying.

Graham Parker, who never lets anything bother him?

I back away. What am I supposed to do? I really need to get to Chloe's house. But I can't barge in there. Graham would never want me to see him cry.

"Come on, Sugar." Frances has followed. She wraps her arm around me and gently walks me back down the hall.

I lean my head on her shoulder. "I feel so bad, Frances. I need Mom to take me to a friend's house. But I can't interrupt her while she's disciplining someone."

Is *that* what's going on? What has Graham done? How could Mom have come down so hard on him that she made him cry?

I freeze and look up at Frances. "Why did she make Graham cry? Do you know?"

She looks away and shakes her head. "I was finishing up Mrs. Parker's classroom. I heard some of what's going on. But I'm sorry, Sugar, I can't tell you."

"Why is she being so hard on him?"

"It's her job, Sugar."

I shove my hands in my pockets and glare at my feet, worried I might cry too. "Doesn't Mom know what she's doing to me? Graham is going to feel weird around me because he'll worry I might tell her things. And that means he's going to do the exact same thing everyone else has done. Disappear."

I sprint down the hall and don't look back.

Confession: My mother is ruining my life.

What Normal Means

We do the normal eight-step departure. The one where we set the school alarm and rush out the double doors before it goes off.

When we've driven several blocks away from school, Mom turns to me. There's a slight smile on her face, like she thinks this is just some normal afternoon where normal things happen and I act normally.

It hasn't been that type of afternoon.

But Mom doesn't pick up on this and starts in with a regular ol' normal question. "So how was your day?"

I press the side of my head against the window and close my eyes. How can I possibly start this conversation? She knew how important going to Chloe's house was to me. It was my chance to turn things around, and now I've blown it. I'll have to walk into the lunchroom and admit to Andrea that she *is* right — parents driving their kids is a normal thing, not a miracle. And in my case, normal never happens. Whatever normal means.

"Four o'clock," I say, my voice gravelly.

She squints at the digital clock on her dashboard. "It's five fifty-seven, actually."

"Four o'clock doesn't ring a bell?"

She winces like she's unsure.

"Chloe. You said you'd take me to Chloe's."

Mom gasps and covers her mouth. "Oh, Allie. I'm so sorry. I forgot."

I shrug, not really knowing what to say now. No matter what, this conversation will either end right now or just get worse.

"Why didn't you come find me?" she asks.

It gets worse.

"I did. You were in Mrs. Parker's classroom yelling at Graham."

"You saw us?"

"He was crying. Why?"

She sighs. "It's complicated . . ."

"Why was he crying, Mom?"

She grips the steering wheel tighter. "You know I can't share a student's private matters with you —even if it's your friend."

"So I have to tell you when my friend is doing something wrong, but you can't tell me anything. That's so unfair."

Mom takes a deep breath. "Allie, I know it's unfair that you are in such a difficult position. It's probably not easy being the principal's kid—"

"Probably?! Try definitely."

"Allie, please—"

"Joel Webber is the only one who should get in trouble. At least you gave him detention."

She tilts her head. "Detention? No. I was letting him get his homework done in my office. The poor kid had a rough day."

"Joel. *Joel* had a rough day?"

"He's a funny boy. You should get to know him."

I clench the fabric of my jacket. That jerk even

has Mom convinced that he's charming. "He's a fake."

"Allie! Don't say that."

"He is. He's mean to me. And Graham."

She tilts her head. "How so?"

Oh, no. I'm not falling for this trap again. "Nothing," I mumble. "Never mind."

We pull into the driveway. Mom turns the car off and faces me. "I wish I could explain what was going on with Graham today. But I can't." I gather my stuff and hug my backpack for a moment. "I am very sorry about not taking you to Chloe's house. I will call her mother, and we'll figure out a time—"

"No," I say sharply. "I don't want you involved in my life."

"But I want to be involved *more,* not less." She tries to reach out for my hand, but I pull away and open the door.

"Mom, you haven't been involved in my life for a long time. Why start now?"

I slam the car door shut.

Whale Talk

Like it?"

Dad shoves a half-carved whale at my face.

"Sure," I say, and slump into a chair in the kitchen. Mom kisses Dad on the cheek, then quietly makes her way upstairs. Within moments I hear the bath water running.

There's a pit in my stomach. Slamming the car door on my mother — the principal — is not a smart idea. The fact that she walked right up the stairs without even mentioning it makes the pit grow even bigger.

"I'm thinking about making it a smiley whale." Dad scratches his head, and his hair pokes out in all directions. "Like it's having a really happy whale of a day. Maybe I'll even carve positive words on the bottom. You know: *passion,* or *fun,* or *joy.* It could be a collector's item — get all the happy whales! Collect all the words! Like it?"

I flop my head on the table. "Love it."

"Tough day?" He ruffles my hair.

I reply with a long moan.

"Go get ready for dinner. Tonight is stir-fry! But it's not fresh, just the frozen kind in a bag, so don't have high expectations. Oh, and your friend Chloe called."

I snap my head up. "She did?"

"Twice."

"What did she —"

"No, wait." He scratches his head more and makes his hair look even wackier. "Three — she called three times."

I hop up and grip his arm. "What did she say? Every single word. Take. Your. Time."

He thinks for a moment. "I told her you were still at school. And she said to give her a call."

"That's it?"

"She also thanked me. Is that important?"

I need details. "Her tone—was it carefree? Or concerned? Or—"

"Just go call her!" Dad nudges me and hands me the phone. "But make it quick. This frozen stir-fry cooks quickly."

Skipping steps, I rush up to my room and punch in Chloe's number. She must have caller ID, because she knows it's me as soon as she answers.

"Where were you? I was getting worried."

Relief rushes over me; she doesn't sound mad. She sounds like she actually wanted me to come over.

"Mom had something after school, and she couldn't take me. I'm sorry. We could talk at school—"

"Wait, hold on, Allie." I can hear muffled conversation. "Okay, I'm back. Mom says when she picks me up after school on Monday, you can come with us to my house then."

My stomach jumps, lurches, spins, twirls . . . everything. It does everything.

Chloe just invited me over, and her mom is

going to drive us. This is amazing. "Are you sure she doesn't mind? That would be perfect."

"Oh, sure. Then your mom would just have to pick you up on her way home from work. School! It's weird, your mom's work is also school."

"Weird. Yeah, I know."

"See you Monday?"

"See you Monday."

I skip down the stairs. On the kitchen table, Dad has set a newly carved baby whale. I flip it over. On the bottom it says HOPE.

Thank you, whale.

I hope to collect them all.

A Royal Exit

My weekend is a blur. Monday is a blur. All I can do is focus on the clock and anticipate the sound of the dismissal bell. *Brrrrrnnngg!* Like a ninja in stealth mode, I make my way to the cafeteria in record time. Hopefully the Afters will get here soon so I can tell them I have to hurry over to the carpool line and catch my ride with Chloe.

I feel a flutter in my stomach when I think of those two words:

Carpool.

Line.

I will finally — for the first time ever — get to stand out in front of the building *like a normal person*.

"Good, I'm glad you're here." Lexa marches into the room. "Lots to plan."

Maddie follows right on her heels, sipping from her orange-juice box. "What if you surprise someone so much that they die from surprise? Is that possible?"

"Google it," Lexa answers.

"Actually, she shouldn't Google that." Graham has flung open the door and joins them midconversation. "The words *surprise* and *die* together in a search would turn up some disturbing stuff. And we are trying to be good role models for Maddie." He bops her on the head. "Your dad is forcing us, kiddo."

"I have to leave," I blurt out.

The room goes quiet.

Lexa finally breaks the icy silence. "But you weren't here yesterday. Graham wasn't either. No one tells me anything."

Maybe this is my window—a chance to ask Graham about what happened with Mom. "Why weren't *you* here yesterday?"

"Does it matter?" He looks around at all of us. "Do you care?"

"Yes," Lexa says.

"Yes," I say.

"My orange juice expires today." Maddie isn't quite following along with the conversation.

Through the cafeteria window, I see a hand waving. It's Chloe. "Let's go!" she mouths to me.

"You guys—I'm sorry. I really have to go." I scramble around to gather my things.

Maddie tugs on my sleeve. "But you can't leave school *now*. The sun is still really high in the sky. What if you get a sunburn?"

This makes me smile. "I'll ask for sunscreen, promise."

"But I have a new Awesomesauce idea." Lexa crosses her arms. "This is one we can all do together."

I rush toward the door. "Great, can we all work on it next week?"

"We have to. Next Friday to be specific— that's her birthday."

I call out over my shoulder. "Whose birthday?"

"Frances, silly." Maddie tilts her head. "You *always* remember."

Oh, sheesh! How could I forget? I'm the one who gets something for her every year; nobody else does. So it's sweet that Lexa wants us all to do something together.

"Sounds great!" I call as the door closes behind me. I join up with Chloe, and we walk toward the front of the school, side by side.

I feel bad about leaving them, especially since Graham might have opened up about what happened with Mom. But right now my insides fill with butterflies as I push through the double doors and do something I have longed for: wait in the carpool line.

Things I Have Never Done

1. Waited for the carpool.
2. Ridden a bike home from school.
3. Grabbed the house key from under a fake rock and let myself in while my parents were at work.
4. Watched a three o'clock cartoon during the school year.
5. Burst through the front door after school and hurried to change into my "play clothes."
6. Been late for school.
7. Felt like a normal kid.
8. Ever admitted this to Mom.

I Don't Know *All* the Rules

So how does this work?"

"Just do what everyone else is doing," Chloe says. "But maybe stop bouncing on your toes so much."

"Stop bouncing. Got it."

The mob of kids stands in a straight line. When a parent pulls up, the teacher calls out the student's name. They step forward, wave to the crowd, get in the car, and their fabulous life gets underway.

"Why is everyone so calm?" I ask.

She shrugs. "It's just a car. Pretty boring stuff."

"Boring?!"

She folds her arms. "Have you ever ridden the bus home?"

"Me?"

She realizes her mistake. "Oh, sorry. But you've at least been on the bus for a field trip. And you know how awesome bus rides are. Can you imagine doing *that* every day?"

It had never occurred to me that the carpoolers might be jealous of the bus riders. I guess that whole "grass is greener" saying is true for school transportation too.

"Carpooling or riding a bus—I'd love to do either one every day!"

Some students look over at me. Apparently I'm not fitting in with their relaxed vibe. I lean in closer to Chloe. "Sorry. I'm just so excited, and I've never . . . wow—the sun!" I shade my eyes. "Maddie was right. The sun *is* bright this time of day."

Chloe laughs. "It's like you're an alien visiting a foreign planet."

I nod eagerly. "I come in peace."

"So who is Maddie?" she asks.

"Maddie is . . . um . . . this girl. She's in second grade. You probably don't know her."

"Maddie Vicario? The teacher's kid?"

"Yeah, that's her."

"She gave you advice about the carpool line? Are you two friends? A second-grader?" She smirks like she's making a joke.

I wave her off. "No, it's more like I babysit her. After school. If she's not with the rest of us, Mr. Vicario won't let her roam around."

"So you roam around with the teachers' kids after school?"

I'm not really sure how to answer this. Even when Chloe and I were friends, I never talked to her about my after-school life. But what else can I say? "Yep."

And now I'm bouncing on my toes again, but this time it's to try to spot Chloe's mom in the line of cars and hopefully get out of this conversation.

Chloe says softly, "Cool."

I stop bouncing and smile at her. "Yeah. It *is* pretty cool."

"Chloe!" Mr. Duncan waves her over.

I'm not sure what to do. My name wasn't called, so technically I should still be standing in this calm, horizontal line. I freeze.

Chloe looks back. "Hurry!" She grabs me by the elbow and pulls me in closer. "Allie's coming home with me."

Mr. Duncan looks at me and holds out his hand. "Note?"

"I need a note?"

Chloe wrinkles her forehead. "Didn't you get your mom to write a note giving you permission?"

I feel my stomach drop. "I didn't know I had to. This is my first time."

Shaking his head, Mr. Duncan announces— quite loudly, I might add— "No leaving with another parent without a note. That's the rule."

My face turns hot. How could this whole wonderful moment be ruined by a rule? One I should know, since Mom *writes* the rules.

Chloe clears her throat and points to Mr. Duncan's walkie-talkie. "You could just call the office," she says.

"The carpool line needs to keep moving," he says.

"Please, Mr. Duncan," Chloe begs. "We need

to go work on our project. Do it for the sake of learning. For the sake of literature!"

A very slight smile appears on his face. He begrudgingly pulls out the walkie-talkie. "Duncan to front office."

There's a crackling noise and then the familiar voice of Mrs. Owens, who works in the office. "Yes, Mr. Duncan?"

"I have Allie West here with me." He looks down at me. I scuff my shoe on the sidewalk. "Does she have permission to go home with Chloe Alvarez? She does not have a note."

In the background, I can hear Mom. "Sorry! Forgot to write one. Yes, let her go, Steve. I mean Mr. Duncan!"

There are some laughs from the line, but Mr. Steve Duncan is focused on the job at hand. He pulls open the back door of Mrs. Alvarez's car, motions for us to climb in, and says, "Have a wonderful afternoon."

Wow.

I feel like the queen of Carpool Kingdom.

Sniff

There is a familiar coconut smell.

Chloe's mom is the manager of the Bath & Body Works at the mall, and she always smells fantastic. Tropical. Her car does too.

"Allie!" Mrs. Alvarez looks at me in her rear-view mirror. "So glad to see you again."

"Thanks," I say. "You too." This small exchange is so loaded with hidden tones. Is she *really* glad to see me? Has she been mad at me this whole time, right along with Chloe? And now is it all just — over?

A girl can hope.

As I fasten my seat belt, I sniff the seat.

Hopefully, they don't notice. But that's how much I love the smell of Mrs. Alvarez and her car.

When she reaches a stoplight, Mrs. Alvarez asks, "So you girls have a book project together?"

Chloe nods. "Yep." She doesn't say it with a lot of excitement. But then again, she could just be hungry. *I* am.

"Allie, your mom tells me you're hoping to make it onto the Pentagon team. Just like Chloe. She was named captain, you know?"

I nod. But it's awkward, because Chloe and I have exchanged only a few words these past few days. My desire to become a member of the Pentagon was not included in those words. Maybe her mom asking this question gives me the perfect opportunity. A start, at least.

"I've been studying hard. I really hope to make the team. Chloe probably doesn't have to study that much." I give her a friendly punch on the arm.

She rolls her eyes. "Yeah, I wish. Mom has me doing *double* homework."

"Chloe worked very hard for that honor. I'm anxious to hear who will be joining her." Mrs. Alvarez shoots Chloe a proud smile, but Chloe looks out the window like this whole thing is embarrassing her.

We turn into their street. "We're home!" Chloe announces.

After we get into her house and pet her dog, Daisy, we make sandwiches and head to her room. But just before we leave the kitchen, I notice a bunch of shopping bags full of stuff in the corner. Streamers. Napkins. Balloons.

The decorations for Chloe's birthday party.

A party I'm not invited to attend.

"Let me know if you get thirsty. And the bathroom's down the hall, on the right." Chloe sounds like a tour guide. Then she flicks her eyes at me. "But you probably remember where everything is, right?"

I give a pretend smile. "Sure, I remember."

But when I look around her room, the feelings I'm trying to hide only worsen.

Seeing her posters and trophies and purple comforter remind me of how things used to be. And what I've missed out on this past year.

Laughing. Sharing secrets. Playing games.

That's what I miss the most — the bizarre games we used to play. Our favorite was Warrior Princess. It involved lots of pretend sword fighting and running and rescuing the wimpy prince because he was always landing himself in trouble. A hockey stick played the role of Wimpy Prince, because no boys would play along.

I was always in charge of the voice-over for the dramatic show — lamely titled *The Wonderful World of a Warrior Princess*. I like alliteration, so the fact that princess starts with *P* and not *W* irked me, but it was the best we could come up with. To make my announcing duties more authentic, I made my own microphone out of cardboard and some black tape that Frances found for me. There was also some glitter, for a fancy vibe.

Our games of Warrior Princess involved tons of drama and swishing sound effects and me saying things like *Will our Warrior Princess ever find her true love and defeat the evil Emperor Dave? And will Emperor Dave finally get that haircut he needs? Stay tuned for next week's episode . . .*

Emperor Dave *always* needed to be saved. He was also pretty boring, as far as emperors go.

What I loved most was that Chloe wasn't embarrassed to play this ridiculous game. In fact, she'd make most of the sound effects—loud and proud—no matter who saw us. Chloe Alvarez is the real deal. Nothing fake about her.

Or at least there wasn't then.

"Let's get started on the project," Chloe says. "I need to catch up on the reading. Do you want to start sketching out ideas for the three-D scene?"

"Just point me in the direction of paper and markers, and I'm in business."

Chloe motions to her desk drawer, then curls up on her bed with the book.

Silently.

This is not exactly what I thought this fabulous experience was going to be like. I mean, I knew she needed to read, but I figured she would do that some other time and we would work side by side, laughing, joking, mending our friendship.

Nope.

It's just me versus a bunch of markers that turn out to be too dry to use. I can't draw anything with these.

I scan the room looking for some other writing utensil. And that's when my eyes land on the top of her bookshelf. Underneath some papers.

Cardboard. Black tape. Glitter.

The Warrior Princess microphone.

She still has it.

Back Then

To be honest, I freak out a little.

Ohmygosh, ohmygosh! Maybe she misses me. Maybe she was hoping I'd see it! Allie, calm down!

Dropping my dry blue marker, I pop up and rush over to the bookshelf. I grab the microphone and hold it up. "You still have it?!" I go into my narrator voice. "On today's episode of *Warrior Princess,* our princess has found herself clinging to a cliff high above a boiling cauldron of hot maple syrup while Emperor Dave, freshly shaven, peers over the cliff and yawns—"

Chloe's cheeks flush. "I never got around to throwing that thing out."

"Throw it out?" My voice catches. I can't

believe this precious piece of handmade equipment that Frances helped me create is something that could soon end up in a landfill.

"That was a long time ago." She turns away from me and gets to reading again. Then she adds in a low voice, "We were so dumb back then."

My stomach drops. Defeated, I just agree. "Yeah . . . dumb."

How could I be stupid enough to think that we would actually pick up our last game like no time had passed? I hope the moment when I apologize will be better than this: natural and magical and just right.

But we aren't getting anywhere. We aren't even working together.

I don't want her to think of us back then. I want now. A *new* now.

So I take a deep breath.

"About the thing that happened last year." I gently sit down next to her on the bed. "The thing with the trading card when you got in trouble—"

Chloe shrugs and stays facing the wall. "Forget it."

We aren't going to do this eye to eye—that's clear to me. Maybe it's better this way. I fidget with my sleeve. "But I can't forget it. Being here in your house, in your room, for the first time in almost a year; it's so hard. Not being invited to your birthday party is even harder." I take another deep breath and close my eyes. "I shouldn't have told on you, Chloe. I'm sorry. I get why you're mad at me."

She sits up and wraps her arms around her knees. "I'm not mad. I just . . ." Her voice trails off.

"You just . . . what?"

Chloe pauses. "I want to trust you, Allie. But I can't. Not entirely." She turns to the wall again, curls up, and continues reading in silence.

Ouch.

I slide back down to the floor and continue working on the sketches, dry markers and all. Except I don't sketch anything for the project. I draw a picture of one very sad owl.

Underneath, I write *Me*.

Confession: Mom's not the only one ruining my life. I am too.

Meaning

Graham is very particular about definitions; he loves to talk about what words really *mean*. He's the one who taught me to pay more attention to the words people use when they have a choice.

For example, my dad works in a shed.

Dad says he works in a studio.

It has the same four walls, the same floor, the same rickety light fixture hanging from the ceiling. But to him, it's a studio, a place of creative possibilities.

I'm trying to see things like he does. I'm really trying.

The sun is setting and Dad hasn't come inside. He's busy gearing up for another craft fair, so we're not even watching basketball like usual tonight. He's probably getting hungry, so I scoop out some spaghetti from the plastic container onto a plate and knock on the door of his ~~shed~~ studio. "Dinner!"

"Come on in."

The room is filled with scrap wood. Dust hangs in the air. Shavings cover the floor. I set his plate next to a half-carved lion and a half-full cup of cold coffee. Dad is wearing a headlamp to get better light on some wood in his hand. He looks like a dentist or a surgeon, except with lots of denim and dirt.

"Have fun," I say as I twirl around to leave.

"Wait. I need your help."

"Dad—I'm starving."

"Bring your food in here. I could use your opinion."

I can't help but love that he wants my opinion—no matter what it is. Within moments, I'm back with my own scoop of spaghetti.

"So this upcoming craft fair is a big deal for me," Dad explains. "I'm told that the head of the

Atlanta zoo will be there, and she's looking for new local talent. They want to feature art from people in the area and put it in the gift shop."

I slurp up a noodle. "Really? How cool!"

"Maybe I could even expand the studio into a massive one. I could have more wall space for hanging all my tools and drawers for all my supplies. And I could install great lighting. I wouldn't have to use this camping headlamp. What do you think?"

I stare at my food. "Sounds great, Dad. It would be nice to have a kitchen table that isn't covered in sawdust." Deep down, though, I love it when the signs of his wood carvings are all over the house. That smell of fresh-cut pinewood means Dad is nearby. "Is that all you needed me for?"

"No, no. Hold on." He grabs a photo off his worktable. "Whatcha think? A meerkat. Kids love meerkats, right?"

Eww. Meerkats are creepy. They look like they're up to no good—like they'd steal the food right off your plate. Or throw sticky food at you for no reason and then act all charming when they don't get their way. Meerkats are the Joel Webbers of the zoo world.

I shake my head. "How about an owl?"

Dad makes a face. "I get it—you love owls, Allie. But I'm trying to figure out what lots of *other* kids would want to buy from a gift shop."

"Owls—they'd want to buy owls! I can't back that up with research or anything, but owls are so cute, Dad. And they have *meaning*."

"Hmmmm . . ." Dad looks up at the ceiling. "I'm going with my gut, my instinct."

"And?"

"It's meerkats." He turns his headlamp back on and studies the photo.

Maybe Chloe would still be my close friend if I hadn't been quite so instinctive. Blurting out Chloe's name when Mr. Vicario asked about the card was my first instinct. I didn't give it any thought, just reacted. Why didn't I take a moment to consider my choices? Hide it. Say I found it on the floor. Take the blame. Any of those would've ended with me still having Chloe as my friend.

I lean over Dad's shoulder. "But what if your

gut is wrong? What if you later decide that you should have taken a moment to think twice? You regret it. But now you can't take it back—"

He lifts his head. "We're not actually talking about meerkats, are we?"

"When I told on Chloe last year for breaking a major rule and bringing a trading card to school, I acted on instinct. Now she says I can't be trusted, even though I apologized. I don't know what to do." I lean my head on his shoulder, grateful that I have a dad whose shoulder I want to lean on.

Dad turns off his headlamp, pulls up two stools. We sit.

"Bill Russell was one of the greatest basketball players in NBA history."

"Dad." I grin. I can't help it. Even though he uses basketball analogies far too much, I have to admit: I kind of like hearing them.

He points to the far wall. A poster. *"The most important measure of how good a game I played was how much better I'd made my teammates play. Bill Russell."*

I sigh. "Meaning . . . ?"

"Stop worrying about everything you've done. If you've apologized and said everything you can to make it right, now you need to act. Focus on how to make things better for other people."

"Got it," I say, like I know what he means.

I don't know what he means.

Hopefully I *will* get it someday, because I can't spend the rest of my life contacting NBA basketball players hoping for answers to life.

There has to be an easier way.

A Sunflower Celebration

I stand tall under the warm spotlight on the stage, feeling very Lexa-like. "I have an announcement!"

Since the NBA pep talk last night with my dad, I've been thinking about how to make things better for other people. The first name that comes to mind isn't Chloe's.

"Frances has a birthday coming up," I say. "Usually I get her sunflower seeds. But this year I want my Random Act of Awesomesauce to be for her. Not a teacher. For Frances. And I want all of you to help me. It won't be anonymous like the Secret Santa, but I think it's even better this way."

Lexa taps on her clipboard and paces. "I'm liking this. Go on."

Graham takes a sip of Sprite. "What will we do?"

"We do her job for her," I explain. "We let her relax. Someone brings her a bag of sunflower seeds."

Maddie hops up. "I'll bring the seeds! And what if I distract her by doing a celebration sunflower seed dance, and I'll wear my T-shirt with the sunflower that has sunglasses on!"

"YES!" Lexa puts a hand on Maddie's shoulder. "Now, stop spinning around so fast. You'll get sick."

I turn to Lexa. "Well? Do you like the idea?"

She grins. "It's perfect."

A Wrinkled Answer

In literature class we read the final chapters of *A Wrinkle in Time*. Ms. Santos leads us in a discussion about the forces of good and evil.

I'm still distracted by everything that's been going on, so I'm glad that Andrea is sitting next to me and keeps raising her hand, which means Ms. Santos won't call on me.

But then she does.

"What symbolizes the good? Allie. Allie?"

I've been spending most of the class staring at Andrea's sparkly blue notebook cover and thinking about instincts, decisions, Chloe not trusting me, sunflower seeds . . . then back to the sparkly notebook. I am *not* thinking about literature.

But Ms. Santos is waiting for an answer.

"Things that are . . . sparkly?"

Laughter erupts like a wave across the room.

Ms. Santos is fond of order, calm, quiet. Not laughter that *erupts*. Usually whenever someone goofs around in class, she sends them to the back desk—the one facing her closet. We call it the Chair.

For a moment, Ms. Santos flicks her eyes between me and the Chair. Like she's figuring out what to do. There are more giggles. It's all weird and awkward as we stare each other down like in a duel in a Western movie.

She takes a deep breath and finally says, "Keep up, Allie. Jeremy, will you answer that question?"

That's it.

That's it?!

The giggles quickly turn to murmurs. I overhear some kids whispering, disgust on their faces.

"*Of course* the principal's kid never gets in trouble. Even for a joke answer."

"So unfair."

I wish Ms. Santos *had* sent me to the Chair.

Tied me to the Chair! As much as I don't want to get in trouble, I really don't want special treatment.

Being an insider at this school only makes me feel like an outsider.

As Jeremy gives his long answer to her question, I push my chair out and stand. Without saying a word, I gather my books and walk straight to the back. To the Chair.

I sit and face the wall.

This is what I deserve. To be treated like everyone else.

After the whispers die down, the class goes back to work. I glance back and notice Chloe is looking at me.

Smiling.

It Happens

It happens without warning.

It happens just minutes before the final bell rings.

Chloe Alvarez slips me a piece of paper.

What you did today was awesome.
Will you come to my birthday party?
It's Friday, after school. I can't have
it on my REAL birthday because
my brother has another swim meet.
Ugh! Hope you can come. My mom
will drive us all. Meet us in the
carpool line.

Please!!!

~Chloe

My Response

Yes.

And for the rest of the afternoon, I float.

My Happiness Is Showing

When I find the Afters, Maddie is doing jumping jacks and counting them off. "Allie! Four. Five. We need you! Six. Seven." When she gets to ten, she stops and isn't even breathless. "You're the one they all love."

"Why? Who? What?" I'm not sure which question I should ask.

"Strawberries. Lexa needs them washed and cut a certain way so they'll stick right on the cardboard and not fall off and get trampled and make a big mucky mess, and I'm out of M&M's. Got any?" Maddie thrusts her empty palm at me.

I tap her on the nose. "Nope." I make my way

toward the stage, where Lexa is sticking her head into a paper bag. "Lexa, can you please translate everything Maddie just said?"

She looks up. "All the strawberries in this bag need to be cleaned and cut so they stick on cardboard."

"You realize that makes no sense, right?"

She sighs. "My Random Act of Awesomesauce. Today I'm making a piece of strawberry art for Mrs. Lee. You cut the tops off and stick them onto the cardboard with pushpins—"

"Like dead bugs!" Maddie interrupts. "I'm trying to make a giant dog nose. For the front of Dad's car."

"Random, but adorable." I reach for Lexa's bag of strawberries. "I'll take them to Ms. Jean. She'll let me use the kitchen."

"Thanks." Lexa studies my face. "What's up with you?"

I wipe my cheek. "Crumbs?"

"You look so . . . happy."

I want to tell her that my world just flipped upside down today—because Chloe invited me to her party. Because I might finally feel like a normal kid.

But that seems like a dumb thing to say. I'm happy because I got invited to a party. Lexa wouldn't understand why it could change my life. And Maddie attends parties only when she knows what flavor frosting is on the cake—which I strangely respect.

"It's just a good day, that's all." I tuck the bag of strawberries under my arm. "Where is Graham?"

"Oh!" Maddie pulls out a piece of paper stuffed in her sock. "Graham gave me this note. It's for you."

Meet me in the nurse's office.

Stop worrying. I'm not sick.

—Graham

Cots and Questions

The strawberries will have to wait.

When I make it to the nurse's office, I'm out of breath. The smell hits me — it's like a mixture of rubbing alcohol and bug spray.

Graham is glancing around the room as though he's measuring. "The cot," he says. "Can you sit on that?"

I'm confused. "Yes. Yes, I can." I sit. Still confused. "Why are we —"

"Hold this." He hands me his music book. "Not like that, like *this*." He opens it and gives it back to me so he's facing the notes on the page. He pulls out his clarinet. Warms up, then starts in with the song.

"What are we doing?" I peek over the top of the book.

"My Random Act of Awesomesauce for Ms. Silk. It's her favorite song, and I need to practice more before I record it. This is the only room where I know she can't hear me. Hold it a little higher, please."

I glance at the upside-down words. "'You Are My Sunshine' is Ms. Silk's favorite song?"

"Hold it higher," he repeats.

When my face is covered and the music fills the room, I realize this is the perfect time to ask. Why had Mom sounded like she was coming down so hard on him?

I wait until he's between breaths. But sometimes my brain and my voice do not communicate, and the question that comes out is unexpected.

"Why do you wear El Guapo's cape?"

Why did I just ask that?

The room goes silent.

Oh, no. Is he mad I know his secret? I duck farther behind the music book.

A finger appears over the top, and Graham gently pushes it down until our eyes meet. "Protection," he says.

I'm afraid to keep asking. But I need to know. "Protection from boys like Joel Webber?"

He shakes his head. "I wish it was that simple. I've already figured out how to protect myself from Joel." Graham dips his head. "It's everything else that I have trouble with."

Even though Graham and I are not-friends, or sort-of-friends, or after-school-friends, or whatever we are, it feels strange to hear him say that.

"Soooo . . ." I hope he'll finish my sentence.

"So, let's get this Awesomesauce project done." Graham lifts the music book back up to cover my face.

I don't ask any more questions.

After a couple of practice runs through the song, Graham stops and packs up.

"Pretty great," I say.

"Now I just need to figure out how to record it for her."

"We do have a digital recorder at this school. And if you've forgotten, I do have connections."

"Thanks, Allie." He leads me to the door and turns out the light. "So now I have a question for *you*."

"Yes, my arms are numb from holding that book."

He laughs. "Why were you smiling so much this afternoon?"

Friend, not-friend, whatever we are—I blurt it out. "I'm invited to Chloe's party."

We walk in silence for a few steps, stride for stride. Then he whispers, "Cool."

Like Furniture

Three.

On Friday morning there are three outfits laid out on my bedroom floor, each a different level of fanciness. School clothes, casual wear, and the dress Grandma made me for my church confirmation last year. The dress has a green satin sash that ties into a huge bow in the back. I might feel like an *actual* present wearing that to a party.

It's hard to know what to choose, because I have to wear it all day at school. Chloe's mom is going to pick us up in the fabulous carpool line again. Which I am a pro at now, and I already have my note from Mom tucked in my backpack. Also in my backpack is my birthday gift to Chloe.

It's not the store-bought kind, since no one had time to take me to the mall. Luckily, Dad is letting me give her one of his carved animals. An elephant. Chloe *loves* elephants. Or she used to. I'm not sure anymore.

I finally put on my favorite jeans and best lacy top, and I even rubbed the dirt off my shoes.

The day goes by in a blur. I spend most of my classes staring at the clock, counting down the minutes.

Finally, *ring!* Last bell.

Chloe rushes up to my desk. "Let's go!"

"I'll meet you at the carpool line," I say.

"Why?"

I'm not sure what to say. Why am I embarrassed that I need to meet the Afters first? If Chloe doesn't want to play things like Warrior Princess, she wouldn't think all the silly things I do with the Afters are very cool. All I've admitted to is *sort of* babysitting Maddie. That's it. So telling her we play Eavesdropping Bingo and run around with stage props on our heads as we do Random Acts of Awesomesauce will probably *not* make her flail her arms and screech, *Please! Be my best friend, Allie West!!*

I cop out. "I have to say bye to Mom first."

"Hurry!" Chloe twirls away from me and practically skips away.

I speed-walk to the cafeteria. All I have to do is tell them I have to go to a party. If Graham thought it was cool, then he can convince the others that it's a reasonable excuse for missing a meeting.

All three of them are already in there when I push through the doors. Lexa is holding a broom, Graham a mop, and Maddie a bag of sunflower seeds.

Lexa grips the broom tightly. "Why are you dressed up? We're cleaning today."

Oh, no. Today is Frances's birthday. How could I forget? I never forget!

Graham's face drops, like he just figured out my situation. "She's going to a party. It's for Chloe Alvarez."

Lexa plants her hand on her hip. "Is this true?!"

I look at my feet.

"No," Maddie says. "You can't go. Today is when I do my sunflower celebration dance. Watch, I've been practicing!" Maddie dances around, not even caring that there's no music.

But Lexa turns away.

I walk up behind her. "Lexa, I have to go. This is really important to me."

"But this whole thing was your idea. How could you forget it? Forget Frances? Forget *us?*"

"You don't understand . . ." I take a breath, and the words spill out. "I want to have friends."

Lexa whirls around to face me. "Really? Then who are *we?*"

"You guys are—I don't know—always here. I mean a real friend. Gosh, that sounds awful. Let me start over."

"No. I heard you loud and clear. The Afters are just here. Like furniture."

"That's not what I mean, Lexa. The Afters are important to me—"

"Go to your party," she says. "But when you

201

get back, the Afters *won't* be here." Her lip quivers.

I turn to Graham, hoping he'll stick up for me. But he looks just as hurt as the others.

My gut instinct tells me to stay.

But I want to go.

After a moment, I decide to ignore my gut.

So I leave.

Voices

Chloe has invited Andrea and Sofia to ride over to the party, too. Since I'm last getting to the carpool line, I have to sit in the only spot available: the seat up front with Chloe's mom.

The other three sit together in the back. They giggle. They poke each other. They point out things along the way. They giggle some more.

Their back-seat gigglefest makes me uncomfortable. What do I do? Turn around awkwardly and try to participate? I decide it's best to just chat up Mrs. Alvarez. We discuss leather car seats versus cloth. It's actually a riveting conversation.

We pull up to Chloe's house, and the first thing I see is the huge HAPPY BIRTHDAY, CHLOE! banner draped across the front door. Balloons flank both sides of the entrance, and a red carpet covers the walkway leading from the driveway to the door.

We all gasp.

Chloe leans forward. "Mom, thank you!"

"Just wait till you see what's inside."

Chloe squeals and jumps out of the car. I forget that I'm feeling left out, and join Andrea and Sofia as we all rush behind her.

Inside, it's basically a Chloe carnival. Streamers, balloons, and flowers—all in purple, her favorite color—fill the house. A table is spread with Chloe's favorite foods, and a chocolate cake covered in candy confetti is the centerpiece.

It is amazing.

I'm a little jealous.

But I push back that feeling because I'm happy to see Chloe so happy. And I'm happy to be invited back into our friendship.

In a way, this party is *our* party.

We hang out for a while, eat food and that amazing cake, then watch Chloe open gifts.

She opens Sofia's first. A gift card to Target.

Andrea's is next. A gift card to Target.

Oh, no. Are gift cards the new cool way to give birthday presents? People don't want actual things?!

Holding my breath, I watch her slowly open my gift. When she pulls away the wrapping, she gasps. "An elephant! I love it!"

And finally I let out the air and breathe like a normal human. Whew. This is a relief.

Suddenly we're all on the couch, and Andrea and Sofia get on their phones.

"Want to make bracelets?" Chloe points to a bag full of craft supplies.

They shake their heads in unison.

She opens a cabinet full of board games. "How about Twister?" She pulls it out and holds it up high, trying to get their attention.

"Sure!" I say.

Andrea keeps her eyes on her phone. "Nah."

This is Chloe's fabulous party? True, the food and decorations are great. But now we aren't doing anything. I think about the Afters celebrating with Frances without me. I shudder. Why did I leave?

I'm almost . . . bored.

Luckily, Chloe notices. She flops down next to me on the couch.

"Andrea and Sofia can make any party lame when they won't get off their phones." She says it loud enough for them to hear, but they're oblivious. Chloe glances at her watch, then turns to face me. "Mom says you're getting picked up pretty soon. But let's have some fun first. Let's play Warrior Princess."

I can't believe it—she said the words *Warrior Princess*. "Didn't you throw away the microphone after I was here the other day?"

"Of course not. Emperor Dave is getting his shoes shined, and he'll be late for his book club meeting. He needs to be saved."

My stomach flips. She kept it!

"Wait here." She hops up. "I'll go get the microphone!"

Shock rushes over me. Chloe *doesn't* think our

Warrior Princess game is stupid. She doesn't even seem to care if Andrea and Sofia hear. She wants me at her party!

Stay calm, Allie.

There are so many things I still want to explain about the incident last year. My attempt at an apology wasn't enough. I have to say more to her.

Now.

I know I should play it cool, but I can't hold this back any longer.

I rush out of the room and stop her just before she heads upstairs. "Hold on. I really want you to understand that I didn't mean to get you in trouble last year. I told on you because I panicked. Mr. Vicario thought it was my trading card. My mom would've flipped if she thought I had broken the ban. And little Maddie—she wouldn't have been able to hang out with the Afters if Mr. Vicario thought I was a bad influence."

Chloe sits down on the bottom step. "The Afters? Like a club?"

"It's not a club. Maybe. It's—I'm not really sure."

Chloe leans forward. "If I had to stay after school every day, I'd definitely start a club. Imagine all the fun."

Relief washes over me. "Honestly," I say, "I wish I'd never seen that El Guapo card."

"It wasn't an El Guapo card, Allie. Didn't you look at it?"

I'm confused. "No."

"It was *La Guapa*. A warrior princess that's half owl, half something. But it's mostly owl. Graham made that card for you."

"For me? But why did you have it?"

Chloe takes a deep breath. "Here's the truth. Graham had been working on it for a long time, and the cards were banned at school before he finished it. He had to get it to you. My job was to slip it to you during recess. He wanted you to get it but not know who it was from. Like a secret gift —an owl with forty-times power. She also shot rainbow lasers out of her wings, I think."

"But why didn't you say anything after I said it was yours? Why didn't *he* say anything?"

"Graham was really upset that the whole thing had fallen apart, and we both knew you would get in trouble if the card was yours. Especially because of your mom. So whatever. I didn't say anything. Nobody had to know Graham brought that card to school after they were banned, and nobody had to know it was supposed to be yours."

"You mean you got in trouble for something you didn't even do? Just to help Graham? And me? No wonder you were so mad at me."

Chloe shrugs and looks at the floor, then stands up. "I'll be right back. You'll be the announcer again, right? Your play-by-play of the action is the best part of the Warrior Princess show."

I smile a little. "The announcer—of course."

Chloe takes the steps two at a time.

I head back to the living room, but just before I walk in, I hear Andrea and Sofia talking. I step closer. Eavesdropping is my jam. Probably part of my DNA. So it doesn't take long to realize they're not talking about what's on their phones anymore.

"So embarrassing for her."

"Right?"

"Chloe was so bummed she had to partner with her *and* invite her over to work on the project."

"I would die if my mom interfered with my life that much."

"Does Chloe even like her?"

"Who knows? I'm sure Allie's mom called to get her invited to this party, too."

A pain hits me right in the heart. The memory of the car ride to Chloe's house, the first one, when Mrs. Alvarez said she'd heard from Mom that I want to be part of the Pentagon. The only way she'd have known that was if Mom *did* call her.

That's why Chloe invited me to her party. Because the principal asked her to.

I back away slowly.

Quietly.

And slip out the front door.

A Shell Station Moment

I storm down the driveway. A billion thoughts attack me like balls on a pool table, all coming from different directions.

I take a deep breath and look up to the sky.

Why? Why is this my life?

I don't even have to wait for Mom. She pulls the car up next to me, reaches across, and pops open the door. She's all smiles. As she drives us home, I lean my head against the window, watching the trees blur past.

I don't say a word.

Mom looks at the dashboard. "We're low on gas."

She pulls into the Shell station on the corner.

That is not where I want to be right now. I just want out of here.

I say, "I'm going inside. To get a root beer."

She nods and motions to the middle console, where she keeps spare dollar bills. I snatch a few and hustle inside, not even looking for root beer. I just wander around, trying to use up as much time as possible so I don't have to be near her.

"Find the root beer?"

I jump. Mom's done pumping the gas already? "Still looking."

And right there in the chips aisle of the Shell mini-market, she has the nerve to ask me the question. "So how was the party?"

So I tell her.

The Truth

I whirl around and face her, my arms folded tight. "The party was horrible."

She tilts her head. "Why's that?"

"I heard them, Mom. They don't know I heard, but I did. *You* asked Ms. Santos to partner me up with Chloe. *You* called Chloe's mother and made her invite me over. *You!*"

"Oh, honey." She bites her lip and turns to look at the chips display instead of at me. "Dad told me what's been going on."

"Dad? Why?!" I shake my head in disbelief.

"He was worried about you. He said you were afraid Chloe would never talk to you again. I knew you'd never come to me again about stuff at school, so . . ."

"So you thought you'd ruin my life."

"That's taking it a bit far. You just need a chance to talk to Chloe. To spend a little time with her again, show her who you are."

"I'll tell you who I am, Mom. I'm the girl who might be friends with Graham, except that we never talk to each other between eight and three. I'm the girl who doesn't tell on people because they would hate me—I learned that the hard way. I'm the girl who doesn't get invited to parties. Sleepovers. Movies. Instead, I get to wear the janitor's sweater when I'm cold. I count cans of spaghetti sauce. And I spend my time with a group of misfits who don't think I even belong with *them* anymore. *That's* who I am." I turn and reach into the refrigerator, grab the closest thing I can find. Gatorade. "I'll be at the counter."

Even as we check out, she keeps at it. "But you love Frances and Ms. Jean—"

"They're not moving up to middle school with me. I need to find some friends my own age."

"That'll be two thirty-four." The cashier says it in a low voice, like he feels bad for interrupting our "moment."

I hand over the cash and head for the exit without waiting for the change.

"Have a nice day," the cashier says.

Yeah, right.

When we're both in the car, Mom turns to me. "Why are you so upset, Allie?"

There are so many things I can say that will answer this question.

Because I want to be a member of the Pentagon, just to be respected.

Because I miss my owl presents.

Because I want to jump on Donny's trampoline before sunset just once.

And because I'm around hundreds of people all day long, but I'm alone.

Completely alone.

Being an insider at school, knowing all the ins

and outs, like I'm part of a secret society—it all makes me an outsider.

Mom reaches for my hand, but I pull away.

"I have a confession, Mom. I *hate* being the principal's kid."

I Know

I can hear Mom sniffling in the other room. Outside, I can hear Dad using his sander in the shed. We all keep to our safe places, not inviting each other in. This is fine by me. It just adds my parents to the list.

I know Lexa is mad at me.

I know Maddie is on her side.

I know Chloe doesn't want to be friends.

The only thing I don't know is what Graham is thinking.

But out of everyone in this entire universe, right now Graham Parker is the only person I want to talk to.

Basketball Can Fix This

Usually, I'm the first of the Afters to arrive at school. But every Monday, Graham and his mom come in early so she can get her supplies ready for the week.

My typical routine would have me warming up in the cafeteria, chatting with Frances as she organizes the cafeteria chairs and kindly offers me her sweater. But instead, I have come prepared: I am wearing a coat.

And honestly, I can't face Frances. I skipped her birthday to go to a party I wasn't invited to.

Mrs. Parker is in her supply closet counting out pieces of construction paper. In the far corner, Graham is on the computer.

"Hi," I whisper to Mrs. Parker.

She steps closer. "He could use some perking up. I don't know what's wrong with him today."

I wink at her. "I'm on the job."

I hold a basketball behind my back, knowing this surprise will lure him away from a computer game. Well, hopefully.

I go closer. Graham is making a replica of the school in *Minecraft*.

"The janitor's supply closet should be bigger," I say, looking over his shoulder at his creation.

He says nothing. Doesn't even flinch that I've suddenly appeared behind him at 7:30 in the morning.

"Can we talk?" I ask.

"Busy."

I pull the basketball out from behind me and drop it in his lap. "First one to ten baskets gets to drink both Sprites this afternoon."

Graham looks up at me. "No."

What is going on? "Fine. Come play basketball with me, or I won't show you the easy tutorial

I found on how to play 'You Are My Sunshine.' On clarinet."

This isn't technically true. I found a video of someone playing the song on a flute. But these details can get hammered out later.

"Fine," he says. "But we have to make it quick before any other kids get here."

"Promise."

No Game

Out on the blacktop, the air is cold and misty. Before I can even explain the rules, Graham grabs the ball and powers toward the basket. He makes a lay-up. Then he catches his own rebound and keeps on shooting as if I'm not there.

I get it. He never intended to play the game with me.

At least this is a good time for me to start with my apology—tell him that I shouldn't have gone to that party. "Look, Graham, I'm sorry about Friday—"

"Don't apologize to me. Lexa and Maddie are the ones who deserve it." He shoots a three-pointer. *Swish!* "But it may be too late."

I pace back and forth. "I didn't mean to hurt you guys, but you have no idea how hard it is for me. How awful it is to have your mom be the principal. How I'm—"

Graham interrupts. "You're not the only one, Allie. You have no idea how hard it is that Joel Webber has been humiliating me for years. It all started when you embarrassed him when he made you that ring out of grass."

"Wait. I embarrassed *him?* That makes no sense—everyone was laughing."

Graham sticks the ball under his arm. It's like he suddenly can't stop talking. "Not at you, Allie. They were laughing at Joel. You ran off on him, and he was humiliated. So he took it out on me. I guess he was jealous of our friendship."

This isn't what I came for. I shake my head, confused. "So you're saying Joel's been mean to you because of *me?*"

Graham shrugs. "I'm sure that's just part of it, but yeah, basically. And when it didn't stop, I decided I was on my own. I wasn't going to pull you into it and maybe make it worse for both of us. So I had to figure out a way to make Joel's words slide right off. I had to act like he couldn't get to me."

I blurt it out. "Is that why you wear the red cape?"

The mist is making his face wet, but that's not the only reason he wipes his eyes. "Remember how you once told me about the meaning of owls?"

I nod. "Owls are the keepers of secrets."

He pauses, then looks directly at me. "I'll tell you only if you'll be an owl for me."

I take a step closer. "Of course."

After a deep breath, he says, "I wear the cape when I'm scared. I wear it on days when the only thing I have to look forward to is hanging out with you guys after school. I pretend I have El Guapo's powers." He drops his head. "But don't tell. Even if we aren't friends anymore."

"What do you mean? We *are* friends."

"No, Allie. The other day, in the cafeteria, Joel didn't fling that huge milkball at the trashcan. It landed on *me.* Everyone laughed and whispered that you would tell on him, but you didn't."

"But—I didn't know—"

"And then at recess. Joel set up Lainey to fling that ball at me. You did nothing."

"I rushed over to you. I . . . tried. You're not being fair."

Graham shakes his head. "I know, Allie. That's the problem. I know you want everyone to forget you're the principal's kid. But deep down I want you to tell your mom. I can't—I can't *ask* you to. I just want you to stand up for me once in a while. But you don't." He shrugs, like he's trying to shake off this whole situation. "Doesn't matter. Some other kid went and told on Joel; I'm not even sure who. But your mom found out and wanted me to tell her what happened. To get the story straight."

Oh, no. That must have been the conversation in Mrs. Parker's classroom—the one Graham doesn't know I saw. "Mom asked you to tell the truth about what happened at recess?"

He nods. "But I refused. If I told her the truth, who would Joel assume was the person who ratted him out? The person with a reputation for that, maybe?"

I look down.

Graham turns back to his one-man game of basketball. *Swish!* "Most people at school probably think we hardly even know each other anymore. But I know you love owls because of your grandmother. I know you're going to miss Frances when we go to middle school. I know you count spaghetti sauce cans with Ms. Jean and you love it. And I know that you want to be on the Pentagon not just because you're good at math, but so people will like you."

I take in a breath. How does Graham know all these things? I've never even told him.

He continues. "And I know that you clean up the messes that happen because of me. But only when no one will know that you might actually want to help me out."

"What are you talking about?"

"The spitballs. All of them. I know it's you. You're trying to get rid of the evidence that I don't fit in. Or maybe it just reminds you that you don't fit in either."

My stomach twists.

Graham stares down at the blacktop, and says in a low voice, "I've decided that I don't want part-time friends anymore. Friends who only stick up for each other when no one else is looking. Who leave as soon as a better friend comes along."

I can't listen anymore. Isn't *he* the one who said we would only be after-school friends? Without glancing back, I turn and run through the mist into the school building, sprint down the hall, and burst through the doors of the cafeteria.

Frances looks up. I'm sopping wet and have a face full of tears. She holds her arms out. "Come here, Sugar. Lemme give you a hug."

As I hug her, a group of bus kids flows into the cafeteria. I can hear some whispers and snickers.

But I don't care anymore. I hug her tighter.

Without Warning

I'm so sorry I missed your birthday, Frances."

She reaches out to tuck my hair behind my ear. "I'm sure you have a good reason."

I look up at her. "No. I don't. I went to a party for a girl who doesn't want to be my friend."

"Aww, Sugar. Sometimes it's hard to tell. Good friends are hard to come by." She lifts my chin and smiles at me. "But when you do find a best friend, you hold on tight and never let 'em go."

And then it all comes at me like an avalanche: the early years when Graham and I were insepa-rable, the adventures we'd go on after school, the La Guapa card he made just for me, how he tried to be just an after-school friend to make it easier for me. So that no one would make it any worse for the principal's kid.

I've been all wrong about Graham Parker. He isn't the number one nobody at this school.

He's the keeper of my secrets.

My owl.

Graham Parker is not just my friend.

He is my *best* friend.

But I didn't even realize it.

No Words

I get through Monday without talking to any-
one else. Not Chloe, not Ms. Santos, not the Jennas, not Ms. Jean. No one.

A couple of times Chloe comes near like she
wants to say something, but I head in the opposite
direction.

When the final bell rings, I rush up to the
office, hoping Mom will see that I really need a
quiet place to be. Wondering if she'll realize that
the Afters don't want me anymore.

But the lights in her office are off. Mom's not
there.

"She's in meetings all afternoon." Mrs. Owens
puts her hand on my shoulder. "Remember? The

229

school carnival is coming up. There's so much planning to do."

I bury my head in my hands, realizing that I tuned Mom out this morning in the car. She told me what she was doing this afternoon, but I didn't listen.

"She says your dad will be here any minute to take you to the craft fair with him. Good luck with it. Should be fun!"

The craft fair. It's today.

The last thing I want to do is smile and chat people up while trying to sell them a hand-carved wooden duck. Or heaven forbid, a creepy meerkat.

A horn honks from the parking space just outside the front doors. I can see Dad's car through the window. His car is loaded up with boxes, and he's smiling from ear to ear.

My wish for a normal life will never come true.

The Package

Unload these boxes and set the animals up three inches apart," Dad instructs me.

This I can do. Physical labor sounds much more enjoyable than having to talk to people. Hopefully he'll let me just replenish stock the whole time.

In the boxes are elephants, tigers, and giraffes. It's almost soothing setting them out, trying to make sure I don't knock any over. Some I put together facing each other, like they're having a deep conversation about zoo life. And what it's like to be super wooden.

Other exhibitors rush around putting final

touches on their booths. Some are going to sell paintings; others, jewelry. The lady next to us is selling fuzzy slippers in all the colors of the rainbow.

"One more," Dad says. He pushes a box my way. On the outside are the words *For Allie.*

"Please tell me these aren't meerkats." I reluctantly open the top. Under the cardboard, I see a package. Wrapped. "What is this, Dad?"

He shrugs. "No idea."

I pull off the wrapping paper and look inside. Warmth rushes to my face. OMG. "An owl? You carved me an owl?!"

"Me? Nah." He winks. "That just arrived from UPS. I have no idea where it came from." He points to the box. "But look some more. Something else may be in there. The UPS driver is very sneaky."

Underneath the packing paper is a stack—a whole stack—of owls!

I scoop them up and look at Dad. "The UPS driver must have worked on these all weekend."

"Probably had to work hard in his shed to fig-ure out how to do the feathers."

I smile. "Studio, Dad. The UPS driver has a studio."

I proudly set the owls front and center. Turns out, I'm right about their cuteness. Customers pull out their wallets when they see those eyes, those wise eyes that are the keepers of secrets.

As I stash money in the metal container, I see a lady approach the booth. Dad tugs on his shirt to smooth out the wrinkles. Clears his throat. Puts on a dashing smile.

"Mrs. Santiago," he says. "I'm so glad you could stop by."

She is wearing an official-looking badge. CHERYL SANTIAGO, RETAIL SALES DIRECTOR, ZOO ATLANTA.

Cheryl touches almost every animal as if she's trying to sense the vibe she gets from each one. I'm fairly certain my dad doesn't take a breath the entire time.

I shoot him a look. "Relax," I whisper.

She taps an owl. I squirm with excitement. "These are utterly gorgeous. They'll fit right in at our gift shop. I'll send over an order in the morning." She sticks a hand out and shakes his. "Welcome to Zoo Atlanta, Mr. West."

She walks off, and I clobber Dad with a hug.

This Gift

When we get home, I place the owl on my nightstand. From my bed, I can see its outline in the glow of my nightlight. This surprise makes my heart swell with happiness for the first time in a long time.

Honestly, it's a feeling I want to share. To give a gift. Right then and there, I decide to do one more Random Act of Awesomesauce. One I will follow through on.

Only now, it's for the Afters. To make things right.

Connections

I place the genie's cap on my head, take a deep breath, and walk one hall over to the fourth grade wing. It's the end of the day, and there are mobs of kids, pushing, jostling, trying to get to the buses or the carpool line.

This is the first time I've been over here in the fourth grade hall when the kids are still here. It's strange to see all your same teachers' classrooms but with different kids spilling out of them.

Luckily, Lexa is taller than most — or her posture makes her seem so — and I spot her right away.

"Lexa!" I call out.

She spins around and spots me. Her mouth drops. She looks left, then right, then charges up to me. "Why are you here? And why are you wearing that?"

I straighten my cap and clear my throat. "I am a member of the Afters. You guys are *not* furniture to me. You are my rock. My reason to look forward to coming to school."

She scuffs her shoe on the floor, thinking this over.

"Nice cap, weirdo!" someone calls out as they pass us by.

"Hey!" Lexa holds up a fist. "Leave my friend alone."

Her brashness, her fierceness—this girl is the definition of awesomesauce.

She bumps shoulders with me. "You, Allie West, look very festive in that cap."

I give her the side-eye. "I look like a weirdo, but I don't care."

She loops her arm in mine. "I'm proud of you, weirdo."

"Come on, friend. We have a Random Act of Awesomesauce to complete." I tap her on the nose. "You're my cruise director, and I need you."

Her smile lights up the hallway brighter than any fluorescent light ever could.

One Very Opinionated Second-Grader

We hustle over to the second grade wing. Again—super weird to be here around all these small people.

Maddie spots us first. She rushes up and wags a finger in our faces. "Why are you two over here? Together? You're freaking me out!"

"We want to—"

But little Maddie Vicario isn't done. "You two were enemies. Allie, you were mean for leaving us to go to a stupid party." Then she turns to Lexa. "And you were mean for kicking her out. Sorry, but it's true. Now. Apologize to each other."

Maddie takes a step back.

Lexa stands up straight. "I'm sorry, Allie.

Maddie's right—I wasn't thinking about what it's like for you. To be the principal's kid. To maybe want normal friends."

I crinkle my nose. "What can I say? I am the principal's kid; it's in my DNA. And I'm sorry too."

Maddie pulls us in for a group hug. She wiggles with happiness. "Gosh, you guys are tall. I can't even breathe!"

This group. My crew. These weirdos are a ragtag, bizarre cast of characters, but they're *my* weirdos.

All that's missing is Graham.

I sure hope I can get him back.

"We have a project to do, girls. And I need your help."

Maddie's eyes grow big. "Oh, like a mystery!"

"No. There's no mystery. I want to surprise Graham. He needs to record his clarinet song for Ms. Silk, but he doesn't have a digital recorder."

Lexa starts bouncing. She's already a step

ahead of me. "Frances. Go find her and get the key to the supply room. Maddie and I will start setting up the band room."

"I'll meet you there," I say. "Five minutes, tops."

The Plan

Frances is just coming out of the teachers' lounge, so I corner her in the hallway.

"Big favor?" I ask, hands clasped together, the whole thing.

She smiles. "For you, Allie Kid? Anything."

"I need to borrow the key to the supply closet in the band room. For just a few minutes."

"Why?"

There are so many directions I can take this. Tell a white lie. Make her think Mom wants the key. But I decide Frances will understand. "Graham wants to give Ms. Silk a surprise gift —a recording of 'You Are My Sunshine' on his clarinet. But he doesn't have a digital recorder, and Mr. Chapelle is gone now so we can't ask him if we can borrow the school's. I want to get the equipment and surprise Graham."

Frances takes the key off her chain and hands it over. "Everyone loves surprises."

Ahhh. Being an insider has its perks.

Back to the plan.

I rush over to the band room.

Lexa is waiting. "We're all set up here. Just need the key." I hand it off, and Maddie and I stand behind her as she opens the door to the supply room.

The room is wall-to-wall electronic equipment. Projectors. Computer monitors. And the recorder we need. Little Maddie strolls around, lightly touching each item. "It's like the school could take over the world from here. Our command center."

A smile fills Lexa's face. "How about we get moving on this Random Act for Graham?"

I salute her. "Yes, Director."

We set up the music stand at the right height. Place the recorder in a perfect spot so it will pick up every note.

When everything is ready, I fold my arms, satisfied that the Afters have pulled together in such an awesomesauce way. Loudly, I announce, "And now, all we need is Graham."

I head out the door and take off down the hall to find him.

And that's when I hear it: yelling.

Graham Parker is yelling.

The Sound of His Voice

Give it back!" Graham's voice is different. Higher. Full of panic.

Just as I turn the corner, I see Joel holding something high above his head. A brown leather clarinet case. Graham's most prized possession.

Kids have stopped on their way out to the bus and the carpool line. I see Andrea, Sofia, and Chloe in the circle of kids gathering around.

"Give it to me!" Graham jumps, trying to snag the case back.

I can't stand back this time. I push through the crowd.

"Give it to him." I lower my voice almost to a growl.

"Here's your stupid clarinet. Go get it." Joel tosses the case in the air.

Graham scrambles, trips, and lands on his knees just as he catches the case. Safely. But then comes the laughter—a giant wave of it.

Oh, no. When Graham dove, his shirt pulled out. And so did his secret cape. The cape of El Guapo.

Someone yells, "What are you, a superhero?"

I rush to Graham's side as he tries to tuck in his shirt—and the cape. "Thank you," he whispers. It all happened fast. Luckily a teacher comes around the corner, so kids scatter.

But this isn't over. It ends today. Right now.

I take all the shortcuts, and within fifteen seconds, I'm standing outside my mother's office.

My Mom, the Principal

I linger at her door. My hands are shaking. What if she believes Joel's side? Or what if she forces Graham and Joel to talk to each other? Apologize. Shake hands.

Graham would hate that.

Just then the door opens. "Oh! Allie."

I breathe in, breathe out. "Can we talk?"

Mom nods and closes the door behind me. This time I want to talk to her as my principal, not my mom.

Mom sits behind her desk. I sit in the small chair in front of her. Then I tell her everything. That Joel has been harassing Graham. That

Graham won't tell on him because he wants to protect me. That he wears a red cape when he's scared.

"But I've been afraid to tell you all this because everyone already assumes I tell you all the school secrets. And I think you kind of like Joel. Maybe you'll think Graham did something so it's his fault. And he'd have to apologize for something he didn't do."

Mom shakes her head. "I wouldn't do that to him. There are reasons Joel is the way he is, but this needs to stop now." She reaches out. "Thank you for telling me everything, Allie. I will protect Graham. You can trust me."

I squeeze her hand tightly. Breathe in deeply. "He's my friend, Mom. My best friend."

Surprise

When we get back to Graham, I'm shocked to see Chloe standing there—wearing the cape of El Guapo.

Graham is smiling. Laughing. Actually laughing. Joel is gone, but a few other kids are lingering. They laugh too—in a nice way.

"Beware!" Chloe announces in a gruff voice. "The wrath of El Guapo can never be contained! Even if you give him detention!"

Then she gasps when she sees me standing there. Next to the principal.

"Mrs. West—I'm so sorry." She pulls the cape off. "I was trying to help."

"You did," Graham says. He takes the cape from her, folds it up, and stuffs it in his backpack.

"Graham," Mom says, "meet me in my office. I want to get you a Sprite."

He salutes her. "Yes, ma'am!"

Mom turns to us. "Girls. I want you to meet at our house this weekend. To get your book project done."

We both nod.

Click-clack. The sound of Mom's heels gets softer as she heads out to the bus area. I'm sure Joel Webber is about to realize he can't charm his way out of everything.

Chloe and I are alone.

I never explained why I left the party without saying goodbye. But it turns out I didn't have to.

Chloe looks at me. "I should have told you the truth. Your mom did help us become partners for the book project. But the invitation to my party was real."

"But why did you invite me?"

"That day in class when Ms. Santos should have sent you to the Chair but didn't. You put yourself there. It hit me that you didn't want any special treatment. I want you to feel like you fit in. Because you do. And I know now that you didn't get me in trouble on purpose last year."

I press my lips together, then say, "What you just did back there for Graham? It was amazing. He's lucky you were here."

"I'm tired of seeing him get picked on too. That's why I told your mom that Joel was the one who got Lainey to fling that ball at him during recess."

"That was you?"

She nods. "But I think Graham wouldn't back up the story. He never tells on Joel."

"He didn't know who told, and he didn't want Joel to think I was the one who ratted him out. I'm not sure if you've noticed, but Graham Parker is a fascinating boy."

She sighs. "He's a good friend to you. You're lucky."

"I've missed you, Chloe."

There's a sparkle in her eye. Suddenly, Chloe puts the back of her hand on her forehead and pretends to be all fainty. "Oh, Emperor Dave! Save me! I also love your sensible choice in footwear!"

"But you're the Warrior Princess—you don't need me," I say in my best narrator voice.

She taps her chin. "True. I'm going to hang from this cliff for now. When I'm bored, I'll save myself. Don't forget to gas up your station wagon."

We both crack up at this.

Chloe throws her arm around my shoulder. "Will you walk me to the carpool line? I'm late, and Mr. Steve Duncan is not going to be happy about me messing up the order. I'm probably in big trouble."

"Don't worry." I grin at her. "I have connections."

Funnel Cakes and Clowns

The night of the school carnival, I gather up Chloe, Lexa, and Maddie. We stand in line waiting to throw beanbags at a wooden box. The Jennas bound up behind us. "We got our invitations! Chloe, look!"

They unfold the matching letters and hold them up: *You are invited to become a member of the Pentagon. Congratulations!*

"Awesome!" I say. I guess those two reading whizzes are math whizzes, too.

Lexa smacks her gum and sticks her hand on her hip. "When did you get the letter?"

"Just a few minutes ago," says Jenna R.

Maddie starts hopping. "Daddy!"

Mr. Vicario walks up to us. There are two envelopes in his hand. "Congratulations, Allie."

My hands shake with excitement. I got a Pentagon invitation! Honestly, I hadn't been thinking about it nearly as much lately. But I am pretty great at math.

"I have one more letter." Mr. Vicario peers around. "But I don't know where he is."

Chloe throws her hands up. "It's Graham, isn't it?"

Mr. Vicario smiles. "Can you help me find him?"

We all search.

Not at the dunk tank.

Not at the snack bar.

He's not even at the clown basketball game.

We find him in the room where they're playing musical chairs. And that's when I hear the laughter.

Woo-haaa-haaa!

Ms. Silk! She's running from chair to chair along with the kids while Graham plays music. "You Are My Sunshine" on his clarinet. We'd never had a chance to tell him about our recorder setup when everything happened, and Frances put everything away. But now Graham had found an even better way to share Ms. Silk's favorite song —with her and a bunch of other kids.

As soon as the music stops and everyone races for a chair, I can't stop myself from snatching the letter from Mr. Vicario and rushing up to Graham. "We made it! The Pentagon. Together. I know you think you don't care. But you accept, right?"

He shakes his head. "Nah. I'd rather play basketball."

"Graham!"

"I'm kidding. I'm kidding. Let's go whoop it up in the Olympiad. It'll be win number five, and the school can freak out, and we'll be rock stars forever."

"Think so?"

"Of course not." He laughs a little. Then in a low voice, he adds, "But maybe . . . maybe we can talk during the day sometimes now."

"No more maybes."

We look at each other and don't say another word. It's as if everything has been filled in. The worry, the strangeness, the questions about what type of friends we are.

The best kind of friends. That's exactly what we are.

Then, like a warm, comforting cup of hot cocoa, the room, the hall, the entire school fills with the laughter of Ms. Silk.

Clown Basketball

Whoa. Whoa. Whoa." Graham spots the basketball game going on in the gym. Little kids are trying to steal a huge inflatable ball from a goofy clown.

"We have to go play." He pulls me out onto the court.

It's hilarious. The clown is one of those mimes who doesn't say anything, just acts goofy. This one has huge red flapping shoes and an oversize suit covered in pockets. The clown keeps pulling stuff out and dropping it on the floor. Tissues. Rubber frogs. Bags of candy.

Bags of candy!

We all skitter around the floor picking them

up. I spy one bag sitting right next to the clown's foot. When I lean over, I see a human-size tennis shoe under the red flapping part of the giant clown shoe.

Keds.

Mom's Keds. The ones she always puts on when she can take off her high heels.

I look up. "Mom?" I whisper.

She winks.

She never breaks character.

Even though everyone is going to think I am a giant weirdo, I don't care. I grab the goofy clown and hug her as tight as I can. Mom is back.

I am the principal's kid.

And I love it.

This Story

This story didn't start with a bouquet of daisies. Or a beautiful sunset. Or even a really nice letter.

But that's how it ends.

It Ends with a Letter

Just before the sun goes down, I open our front door to watch the sunset. And that's where I find the daisies. And the letter.

From Graham.

> Allie,
>
> What you did for me by standing
> up to Joel and telling your mom the
> truth — it's everything. You were
> courageous. Something I'm going
> to start being too, cape or no cape.
> Maybe I'll say something instead
> of letting everything roll off me.

During the summer, when there are no Afters, we should start up the Creek Club again. Maybe even invite Chloe. And Lexa. She can make an agenda and carry a clipboard. We'll use the wild part of our imaginations in honor of Maddie, and we'll just make it all up. Let's tell stories about alien visitations and teachers turning into zombies and how there are never enough M&M's in the world.

It'll be festive.

I'll bring my clarinet and play "You Are My Sunshine." Because it's your song too.

— Graham

My 3-D Scene

The daisies go in a vase on my nightstand, right next to Dad's owl.

The letter from Graham goes in the box under my bed, along with Grandma's drawings.

I can't wait to hear Graham play "You Are My Sunshine" on clarinet again.

If my life were a book project, this moment would be my 3-D scene, the one where I change the most.

I might have made this a confession once, but not anymore. Now I will say it loud and clear: My life — as an After, the principal's kid, an insider, and an outsider — isn't normal at all.

And that's just the way I want it.

ACKNOWLEDGMENTS

This story began with a reader. At one of my school visits, where I had shared my path to becoming a published author, I told the students that I had grown up as the daughter of the school principal. They heard how that experience—being friends with staff, knowing every single inch of the school, feeling like an insider *and* an outsider—had hugely influenced my writing. After the presentation was over, a sixth-grader approached me. She bounced on her toes. Her smile beamed. In a soft voice, she confided, "I'm the principal's kid too."

"So you understand me," I said.

"Thank you," she whispered, and then she ran off.

I later told a friend about this encounter, and she said, "You must write that story, for you *and* for her. You could call it *Confessions from the Principal's Kid* or something. Just start writing—now!" So I did. This novel is not a memoir nor an autobiography, but it was inspired by my experiences as an After. Yes, I did hang out with a group of kids after school, and we explored and played games and knew which teachers had the best snacks. Yes, I counted spaghetti sauce cans with the cafeteria manager, Ms. Jean. And yes, I wore the janitor's sweater when I was cold.

I always listen to this friend when it comes to writing, because she also happens to be my literary agent. So my first big thank-you goes to you, Jill Corcoran, for always steering me down the right path, even when it seems scary. I'm thinking about getting you some pompoms, because you are the *best* cheerleader —in a booky sort of way.

Huge thanks to my editors, Jeannette Larson and Adah Nuchi, for your guidance and remarkable wisdom. I hope to someday make a giant airplane banner that covers the sky and says THANK YOU, HOUGHTON MIFFLIN HARCOURT TEAM. YOU ROCK!!! (That may be too long and too expensive, but just know that I would totally do that.)

My critique partners and early readers of this novel were invaluable. Thank you, Eve Porinchak and Amy Thornhill. My favorite West Georgia Regional Library Director, Roni Tewksbury, was also a cheerleader for this novel; your support has meant so much to me.

I'd like to thank the teachers and staff members at Mountain Park Elementary in Roswell, Georgia, who helped raise me, fed me snacks every afternoon, and made my after-school life so wonderful: Frances Drizzle, Mr. Reese, "Ms. Jean" Wood, Diane Myers, Pat Owens, Marie Shelton, Cecile Easterling, Dorothy Macris, Joann Simpson, Karen Weaver, Sonia Terry, Ann Ferrell, Karen Cox, Eloise Barron, Kathryn Samples, and Doris Robertson.

Finally, I thank Mrs. Clarke — my principal, my mother, and my best friend. Yes, it was exhausting to sometimes arrive at school in the dark and leave in the dark. But you taught me the value of doing one's job with dedication, passion, and integrity.

Which brings me to this one last confession: Mom, I will forever be comforted by the *click-clack* of your heels getting louder and louder when you walk down a hallway — because it means you're about to peek around the corner and give me a smile. You are my sunshine.